The Accidental Romantic and Other Short Tales

John Devlin

Contents

The Accidental Romantic

Generally, Charlie Bell was an accidental romantic, as in romance usually happened to come to him from time to time through no fault of his own. He admitted as much and when he was in reflective mood he would claim that any woman he had ever been involved with had picked him up. He seldom made the first move, although he definitely wasn't unwilling.

Some of those accidental encounters were all entirely above board, but at times there were also entanglements with ladies of the night. He was the ideal victim as he was always completely unsuspecting, even sometimes appearing to verge on innocent.

One night, he and Big Joe Doyle were in a bar which was swarming with hookers. Everyone was having a great time and during the course of the evening he turned round to his friend and asked perfectly harmlessly, "Aren't there a lot of very friendly girls in tonight?"

The first time Joe saw one of these accidental encounters Charlie and himself were sitting outside a bar in Guangzhou drinking beer. It was late and they were about ready to leave when a tart arrived and started cosying up to Charlie. Joe had seen this lady before and knew she was on the prowl. Joe sat a minute but then realised that Charlie was interested as he went inside to buy her a drink. Joe decided to take himself off and be actively absent as the situation developed.

Charlie was shy about discussing his dealings with hookers. At least he was with Joe. But not with another friend – Denis - who would then relay the stories to Joe. Charlie was drinking with Denis one night when he revealed that the night before, he had got drunk and by mistake had taken out 5000 RMB (about £600) from the bank. As he was withdrawing the cash he had been befriended by two ladies who were lurking nearby. The next thing he knew they were off home with him in a taxi.

When Charlie got home he spent a few hours in bed with one of the aforementioned ladies. Whether he expected a threesome or not is open to question but according to him one lady never entered the bedroom. Sometime during the night his curiosity got the better of him and he went to look for the third person, the Unholy Ghost. He found her on her knees, but she wasn't praying, she was scrubbing the kitchen floor. He thought it better to say nothing and went back to bed with the other lady.

When Charlie rose in the morning, the house was spotless. Everyone was very happy with their night's work. However, he didn't tell Denis how much he had contributed to their pension funds. Forever after, Denis referred to these types of lady friends as "cleaners."

While most of Charlie's mishaps and misfortunes could be laid at his own door, Joe did indirectly bear some responsibility for one episode which eventually led to Charlie getting married. Joe had originally met Charlie, Denis and several other mature students from Ireland shortly after he arrived in Guangzhou. At the time, Joe was settling into his first teaching job there.

This crew had been studying Chinese at a local university and had just completed the course, but some didn't want to go home. In short, they were looking for work. Joe wasn't long accelerating

Charlie's job prospects as he was eligible for a bonus if he recruited new teachers. In the end he collected the bonus for both Charlie and Denis. Charlie was processed much earlier than Denis and sent off to Thailand to do a TEFL course, fully paid for by the company.

As one would have expected, the bold Charlie wasn't long in Thailand before he was befriended by a young lady named Thelma and an amorous relationship followed. However, Charlie's new lover had a friend by the name of Kanda who took a shine to Charlie after a while and asked Thelma if she could take him over. Charlie wasn't consulted, but an agreement was reached between the ladies and the saga of Charlie and Kanda began.

Charlie was in Thailand for two months, first a month of training on Ko Samet island and then a further month while he waited for a visa to get back to China. During that time the relationship with Kanda obviously took off, she looked after him well and he was brought to visit her family. He spent the second month in a hotel in Rayong and was with Kanda virtually 24/7 seeing as he had nothing else to do at the time, just wait. During this time, Kanda got her claws well into Charlie.

The relationship continued after he returned to China. He visited Thailand a few times and after about a year they decided to marry. The first time he announced the impending nuptials was to a group of students and teachers one night in Starbucks. Some of the female students were very excited and asked him many questions about the future wife, how he had met her and whether she would move to China. There were requests for pictures and then oohs and aaahs as Charlie showed them a series of images.

Charlie was also very excited at the time. About a week later he and Joe were in Starbucks, just the two of them, and he spoke about getting some more work as he would need extra money to support a wife. He thought he might join a church or religious group. He had done this before. He planned to join and attend services very regularly until he had got to know the members of the congregation. Theoretically, when he had gained their trust, lots of little jobs would follow.

On Chinese New Year, everyone had ten days holiday and Charlie went off to Thailand to be married. He was gone before anyone knew it, without fanfare, and after he went nothing more was heard from him. He didn't answer texts and remained incommunicado all the while. Every few days, Denis would ask Joe if he had heard anything, but there was nothing. They figured all must be going to plan.

Finally, he resurfaced. Joe had been in Shenzhen for a few days and was on a train home when Charlie called him. He had just arrived back and was now married, but his wife wasn't with him. He would go back for her in six months' time.

Joe rang Denis, who had lots of questions about Charlie which Joe hadn't thought to ask. Later, Joe had dinner with Denis, who still wanted to know all about the wedding. Joe still didn't have the answers but was able to tell Denis that they would meet Charlie later for coffee.

In the evening, after work, Denis and Joe hurried off to Starbucks in great anticipation. They saw their Swedish student Jasmine in there and joined her. After a while, Charlie arrived. He was unshaven and wearing a flowery shirt and a brown leather Jacket. He was in great form and regaled them with tales of the wedding and the parties and his brothers and Kanda and her father and her mother and all manner of other people.

When Charlie had arrived in Thailand, he firstly did whatever he had to do as regards paperwork for the wedding. His brothers had come over from Ireland and with them he went to a resort which he described as paradise. The brothers were totally in awe of this place.

After spending time in paradise, they all set off in a minibus for another destination 12 hours drive away. This was where the wedding was to be. Charlie thought they had booked the vehicle for themselves, but no, the bus was full of unknown people.

They went to a venue where they met a big gathering of people, and Charlie wasn't sure what was going on. There was a huge party where they ate two pigs and countless chickens. This went on for a long time, and Charlie was constantly wondering if he was now married or still single.

Over the next few days, more ceremonies followed. One in particular had impressed Charlie. It was at a temple filled with statues of animals. There were monkeys, elephants, tigers, lions and so on. Again, much food and drink was consumed, but he was never made aware at what point he got married officially.

He also referred to a three pig party he attended at some other juncture. Again there were many chickens consumed at this do. Denis reminded him that Jasmine was a vegetarian. It didn't deter him because he then described how he was first introduced to the live animals before they were dispatched and eaten. He said the Thais even kissed the chickens before they wrung their necks. Jasmine didn't know whether to laugh or cry.

Everyone wanted to know about Kanda's family. What were they like? Charlie said they were fine but he wasn't sure who was who as so many people were described as uncle, auntie, mother, father, brother and sister. It did appear that the father was a builder, "Mr Somewhat" and that his answer to everything was, 'It doesn't matter.'

"Good morning, Mr Kanda!"

"It doesn't matter."

Mr Somewhat also had a manservant who would go off and do shopping for him and also fetch alcohol when required. This manservant rejoiced in the name of "Go for beer" and he was in the habit of taking a lot of drugs, according to Charlie. Charlie guessed there were many people described as aunts, uncles and close relations who were probably just friends.

Questions were asked about the mother but Charlie said he wasn't sure about her or her circumstances. She didn't attend the wedding and was based in another province apparently. He had been taken to visit her on a previous visit but she didn't seem to approve of him. He said that she lived with a crowd of young girls all of whom Kanda referred to as sisters. Charlie harboured a suspicion that she might have been running a house of ill repute.

Then Charlie brought out their presents. Denis got a very colourful t-shirt and a thing that could best be described as a golliwog. Joe also got a golliwog and a sarong with a butterfly on either side of it. Charlie maintained that ladies loved these sarongs and Joe could give it to a favourite lady as a present. Jasmine thought it was all very funny. Joe was wondering if her father, the Swedish Consul, would get to hear of all these carry-ons. Joe was considering whether he should give the sarong to his friend Maggie.

Charlie and Denis had been sharing an apartment up to this point and so there was always news about Charlie's latest escapades. However, after the wedding, Charlie moved to Huadu, which was a remote suburb of Guangzhou and without foreigners. Charlie loved that aspect of life as he was able to practice his Chinese daily. But now there was very little known about his activities apart from what he told himself.

Before moving to Huadu, Charlie had become very friendly with a Chinese guy called Prince, who seemed to be some kind of small businessman. Prince did little to aid Charlie in keeping to the straight and narrow. He may not have led him astray but he kept him in a perpetual state of being astray.

Charlie wouldn't see his wife for six months and so out of sight was out of mind as he carried on his bachelor lifestyle. One night, Denis, Joe, Charlie and a few others were having a drink after work and Charlie described Huadu and the bicycle shop there which was a local meeting place. In the evening, large crowds of young men would gather; there was a brothel next door and the rate was 50 RMB (£6) for 12 minutes according to Charlie.

In this world that Prince had introduced him to he described the two different types of girls available. There were the laughing girls and the sleeping girls. The laughing girls were divorced ladies. Prince reputedly had three of them on the go and did support them in various ways. The sleeping girls were the "50 RMB for 12 minutes" ladies and all the young men of the district availed themselves of their services.

Charlie then started to describe going to the local barber. After the hair was cut and dried the customer would be wheeled into a back room for extra services which were all included in the price. Just as he was about to get into the juicy details, a couple of female students joined the company and that story remained unfinished.

Charlie was always losing things, even money, and a while after he came back from Thailand, he complained of losing 5000 RMB. Denis and Joe were speculating later on what could have happened. They knew he sometimes took out money late at night when he was drunk. They recalled the two hookers watching him withdraw money one night previously before coaxing him into going off with them. Deja vu!!! Then of course there was the fool and his money; another possibility was that he had just lost it. Denis also introduced a third scenario; Charlie may have given bank details to his 'wife' in Thailand and she could have been helping herself. He was already sending her monthly payments.

A couple of months after the wedding, Kanda arrived in Guangzhou. She stayed with Charlie for a few weeks, but he didn't bring her out or introduce her to his friends. After a while she left because Charlie claimed she couldn't settle in China. Whether she had a visa to stay longer was another question.

A few months later Charlie left Guangzhou altogether and took a job in Shenzhen. On his last day he just rushed off telling Joe he had a van waiting for him into which would go all his belongings and which would then move him to his new abode down there. Prince had organised the move and the new apartment.

Later that evening, Denis told Joe a different story about Mr Charlie and the van waiting for him. Charlie had apparently spent the last few days with a tart he had met in The Harp and Shamrock. Every day he had been saying he had to go home early to pack. Denis laughed and said he knew the 'packing' he was doing. He believed that Charlie had fallen for this lady. She had even answered Charlie's phone once or twice when Denis had called.

Not only that, but Denis had also become aware of another mystery lady known to Charlie. This one had been around a while before but had disappeared for several weeks and left all her belongings in Charlie's apartment. Now she had reappeared and told him she had been in jail. Denis didn't get to hear the outcome of that episode either.

The first day Charlie arrived in Shenzhen, he texted Joe in the evening to tell him he had landed safely and was settled in. He had already been out for a spin on his bike.

Two days later, he went on the tear and woke up in a nightclub at 7.00 am. He had fallen asleep in there and the staff just left him to sleep it off.

After that they didn't hear from Charlie very often, but he still arrived in Guangzhou from time to time and on one of his visits he gave Joe a rundown on life in Shenzhen. Kanda had been to visit him there and he was sad about her going back to Thailand. However, he didn't stay long that day as he was off to visit his muse, Prince, in Huadu.

Charlie continued to make regular visits to Thailand to see Kanda. He was sending her money every month after the marriage and there was a house under construction which he was paying for.

As time moved on, the only contact was the odd phone call. Charlie got to know people in Shenzhen, he got involved in different activities involving art, music and poetry. He developed new interests in kites and drones and talked about starting a band with some other foreigners.

As well as his visits to Thailand, Kanda visited Charlie regularly when he moved to Shenzhen, but she never stayed long. He was always lonely when she left and what kept him happy was planning his next visit to Thailand.

Joe met him again after one of these trips and he was in a buoyant mood. He had his big new house nearly built and it was looking good. He had also bought a fish farm for Kanda's brother.

He then talked about the people there. The man he used to think was his father-in-law was actually his brother-in-law and so on. This was the man he always referred to as "It doesn't matter" as those were his only three words of English but were also words which summed up the Thai attitude to life.

There were many kids running around too and he said he was never sure who they belonged to as they were fed and cared for on a communal basis. This all took place in the north of Thailand and apparently, the menfolk all headed south for work and sent money home. Unfortunately, sometimes they got overtaken by events, never returned and the money from them dried up.

He then talked about the Thais cooking for him separately and not letting him eat their food for quite a while because they thought he couldn't take it. Gradually, he coaxed them into letting him eat their specialities.

Joe asked him how his marriage was going given that he was here and Kanda was in Thailand. He said all was fine as far as he knew but oddly suggested that he didn't know if she had a man in Thailand and that there was no point thinking about such things.

Joe had never heard him talk about it like that before but maybe he wasn't feeling too good about things that day or he had some sort of premonition. He was now off to Thailand at the end of January and would visit Kanda's home place this time. Little did Charlie know that this was to be his last visit and that disaster was waiting to strike.

Charlie went over there in great anticipation as usual and everything was going swimmingly for a few days. Then one night they were at a party and he got drunk. There was another man lurking around there and who Charlie supposed was a friend of Kanda's. Anyway, Charlie must have said something to tip the balance because Kanda lost it with him.

There was a very big row during which she revealed that the man who had been hanging around was her boyfriend. The lad started up his motorbike, Kanda jumped on behind him and they rode off into the darkness. Charlie never saw her again, nor the house, nor the fish farm.

All gone in the blink of an eye!!!

Come on, The Corrs

While the world was celebrating the millennium, I was working as a bricklayer in Wimbledon and there I encountered two of the rarest characters, the Killoran brothers. To use the popular lingo among building workers, they were 'Plastic Paddys', born in England but with parents from Ireland.

Big Jim was the older of the two, and indeed, he was something else, to coin a phrase. Desperate Dan would not have held a candle to Jim. Timmy, on the other hand, wasn't as big or as boisterous and was affectionately known as "Timmy the Fish" mainly due to his capacity for liquor.

Jim wasn't someone you became friends with at the drop of a hat. While I always got on well with him, it was a kind of long-distance relationship. Timmy was different. He was a small, shy, ruddy-faced lad who blushed very easily. He rode a motorbike and sometimes came into work on it. You always knew when Timmy was approaching by the roar of the engine. He had a hole in his silencer.

Timmy invariably went to the pub at teatime (11.00 am) and would usually drink 4 pints of bitter. He would have more at lunchtime. If he had brought his motorbike to work, he only had two pints at teatime and none at lunchtime. Timmy talked to me quite a bit once he became familiar with me and after a while he confided that he was Big Jim's brother. That was a surprise at the time as the two of them seldom fraternised, at least at work. Timmy may have been a little embarrassed by Jim's carry-ons.

Jim was about two metres tall, aged about 45, a bachelor and as ignorant as hell. He was built like the proverbial brick latrine with a bullet head housing two small eyes set close together like the headlights on a tractor, overlooked by big black bushy eyebrows which met in the middle. He loved to think he was really cool and always dressed in designer joggers or shorts. He didn't speak much except to give out and usually the only audible words were 'fuck fuck.........'.

When he was on the job, Jim was mad for work and almost always worked on his own. If he ran out of materials, he would hurl abuse at the hod carriers in a very loud voice. He would accuse them of being "paedophiles" which was his way of addressing anyone who aroused his displeasure.

He didn't mind the dirty or awkward jobs as long as he was left alone. The brutally heavy, six-inch and nine-inch blocks, which most bricklayers would run a mile from, were meat and drink to Jim. He would break blocks like biscuits and, when in a bad mood, would sometimes throw broken blocks and other rubble down from the scaffold irrespective of who was walking around below. This would always be accompanied by a string of profanities and references to child abusers.

Foremen gave him a wide berth and they didn't have to go near him anyway, as he hated being idle and would find work for himself. He boasted that when he had been working for Swift Contractors sometime before, the foreman Tipperary Tommy once said, "if I'm ever going to sack you, I'll do it by phone."

Jim's passion was his radio and he had it on constantly. He loved to listen to pop stations and knew all the current artists. He had his favourite singers and bands which he would sing along with. When one of these came on, he would shout, "Come on The Corrs" or "Come on, Brucie, sing it" in reference to "The Boss." He was also known to break into the odd Irish rebel song.

It really annoyed Jim when the advertisements came on the radio and he claimed it was a waste of his money and would shout obscenities at the radio for the duration of the ad. He also got really worked up by DJs or others talking on his radio. If they continued talking for a prolonged period of time he would fire all kinds of verbals at the radio.

Jim maintained batteries cost him £13 every week, but what he didn't realise was that when he went off anywhere, the other lads used the radio. Consequently, he often found it powerless when he came back. One time the batteries gave out during one of his favourite numbers and in a temper, he threw the radio off the scaffold smashing it to pieces on the ground below. A new radio then had to be purchased when he had settled down.

Most building workers go for a fry-up of bacon, eggs, fried bread, beans etc at breakfast time but not Jim. He loved burgers and would have three of these every morning and was very fussy about his order. One of the lads would go to the burger joint and fetch the food for all those who ordered. If Jim's order wasn't exactly as expected he would go bananas.

One day, the burgers were delivered without onions and he threw over the table in the canteen and kicked a chair across the room. Then he said to the messenger, "Tell that darkie I'll be round if she fucks up that order again." Sometimes someone might suggest that he try something else for a little variety, but he would have none of it. Not only did he dislike the fried breakfasts, but he would also get into a lather at the mention of Indian curries or Chinese food. Sometimes Jim would go on the tear and wouldn't be seen for a couple of weeks. He would come back telling great stories of how many cops he had beaten up and how they were afraid of him. At these times, he was known to feast on crates of Carlsberg Special. He was currently on probation for some ruckus with the police and he used to give out yards about his probation officer who he referred to as a "silly cow".

Through time, Timmy filled me in on the family background. There were several siblings, with Jim being the oldest and Timmy quite a few years younger. Timmy, like everyone else, was a little in awe of Jim. He was also wary of the big man as he had seen him in action on enough occasions to know to give him a wide berth when there was trouble brewing.

Timmy revealed that there was another brother, Harry, who had died tragically about two years before when he was involved in a motorcycle accident. Like Jim and Timmy, he was also a bricklayer. Harry was built like Jim but wasn't quite so aggressive, according to Timmy. While he was alive, Harry had been a modifying influence on Jim, but since his death, Jim had got wilder.

When they were all younger and living at home, Timmy recalled Jim and Harry making sandwiches every morning to bring to work. Each of them needed a full sliced pan. But such was the appetite of the two lads, neither trusted the other and they both took their loaves to bed in case the other would steal them.

The Killorans were staunch Irish republicans and Timmy recalled Harry having a girlfriend from Northern Ireland. It turned out she was a Protestant unionist. This greatly disturbed Jim and whenever the girl was in the house, he refused to enter the living room and would march up and down the hall whistling the Irish National Anthem.

Timmy went on to tell me that Jim had two kids who lived with his ex-girlfriend. I knew this already as I had often heard Jim talk about his son, the daughter not so much. He loved the son above all else, according to Timmy. Even his radio! Timmy often saw the kids but unlike Jim he tried to treat them equally.

Timmy went on to tell me that one day, before the son's birthday, Jim went into a toy store down the street from the job in Wimbledon and bought the boy a top of the range scooter with all sorts of bells and whistles. It had been priced at £120, but Jim refused to pay more than £100 and the terrified assistant just gave it to him at that. Jim went off home that evening delighted with himself.

The next day, Jim arrived into work breathing fire. He was like a demon. When the scooter had been presented to the son the previous evening an awful row had erupted between the boy and his sister over the scooter. The boy hit his sister on the head and the mother sensibly decided to put the scooter away. This didn't please Jim who was adamant that the ex-girlfriend, the "bitch", should have explained to the daughter that it was for the boy and no one else.

Jim didn't give the full story, but Timmy knew what had happened and I heard his account the next morning. As the scooter was being put away Jim intervened and a fracas broke out between himself and the kids' mother. In the pandemonium, the scooter fell on the ground and the two adults fell on top of it. The police were called, Jim was escorted away and the scooter was reduced to a heap of scrap.

"That's Jim for you," said Timmy resignedly.

Café en Seine

The tryst was set for Dublin's Café en Seine at two o'clock on Saturday. Mick Ryan took a train from Tullamore and then a tram into Dublin city centre. It was early, so he decided to get off in Smithfield and walk through the city centre. He passed through the fruit market, crossed Capel Street and then dallied a while in the Jervis Centre and Arnotts Department Store, killing time and avoiding the rain.

When the rain ceased, he left Arnotts, cut back down onto the Quays and crossed the Liffey at the Halfpenny Bridge. The route then took him down through Temple Bar, past the Palace Bar and on round by the Bank of Ireland, Trinity College and up Grafton Street. He dawdled for a few minutes looking in shop windows for he was still early. As he arrived in Dawson Street, it had begun to drizzle again, and he went directly into the Café en Seine.

Mick had been here once before and had liked it. It was a very spacious establishment. By night it was frequented by throngs of millennials, posers and hipsters. In the daytime, the atmosphere was much more relaxed, even sedate. Old ladies came in for afternoon tea, couples brought their children in to feed them, and of course, casual lovers would meet there too.

Cafe en Seine in 2008 could have best been described as an emporium serving all kinds of alcohol, soft drinks, meals and snacks. The ground floor consisted of a very long narrow area with lots of nooks, crannies and alcoves off the main bar. There were large areas upstairs too, but Mick had never had reason to venture up there. It was wonderfully decorated in vibrant colours. It was possible to take a seat if you were on your own and quietly blend into the background. There were lots of statues of humans and animals, busts, urns, columns, exotic plants and huge glass orbs hanging from the ceilings.

On entering, Mick walked through to the far end, looking into every corner where people were, checking if Emma was already present. As expected, she still hadn't arrived, and so he ended up back by the front door. He positioned himself behind an urn which had a huge palm type plant growing out of it. A smiling foreign waitress approached after a while to enquire if he would like to order, but Mick assured her that he was waiting on someone. As a concession, he did allow her to bring menus.

A blonde lady came in, and at first, he thought it might be his internet date until he noticed that she was accompanied by a man. He texted Emma at the appointed hour to announce his arrival, but he might hardly have bothered. She arrived almost immediately and walked straight up to him. Mick beckoned her to take a seat, but she didn't. Emma kept walking all the way along until she arrived at the bar, where she pulled up a stool and sat down.

There was nothing else for Mick to do but follow, abandoning his carefully chosen table. When she had decided on her seat, he sat down on the high stool next to her. She allowed him to get her a Sauvignon Blanc. He decided he would have one of those as well, even though it wasn't a drink he would habitually order. They were both giggling and laughing and soon were involved in a long conversation about life, love, the universe and a multiplicity of other unrelated issues.

The wine went down well and they had another. Then they decided to have lunch. It was raining outside and they thought they might as well eat where they were, but at a table. They settled on a spot next to where Mick had originally been seated but without the protection of the large urn and the overarching palm plant. He did mention to Emma that they might have sat here originally, but she dismissed this idea and said it was a lot better to sit at the bar. In her opinion, it was much more close up and personal, and she wanted that to start with, so she could get a good look at him.

Emma went outside to smoke, and he accompanied her. It was still dull and cold and definitely not summery. Emma didn't seem to feel the cold. Mick was wearing a shirt and jacket, but she was only wearing a flimsy top and didn't seem to notice the cold at all. She smoked, and they drank.

A Romanian gypsy appeared and put her hand in across the barrier which separated the cafe from Dawson Street. They were so caught up in themselves they ignored her, but the people next to them contributed. A couple of minutes later, a second beggar arrived and made a beeline to the previous contributors. Mick and Emma watched with interest. Emma said she never gave money to beggars as the first receiver would send another to you and another and another... until you would have to leave.

They went back inside and their table was still free so they ordered food which soon arrived. They both had a burger which came with the standard chips and salad. It looked good, and they both treated their food to large dollops of mayonnaise and ketchup. Emma had more wine, but Mick had tea this time. They were talking a lot and the food went down easily. Mick then had a dessert and more tea, but Emma declined, although she did have another Sauvignon Blanc. And they talked more. It must have been the alcohol talking, but Mick did happen to mention at this point that he considered Emma to be a very pretty lady, that he liked her and would love to get to know her better. Not a full-on declaration of love but a precursor of sorts. She thanked him.

They talked about trains and getting home to Tullamore and Drogheda, respectively. Then out of the blue, she casually mentioned that she would like to go to bed with him at some point in the future. They went outside again while Emma had another cigarette, and again, the beggar approached them and was very persistent. This time Mick called a waiter who saw the beggar off, at least temporarily.

It was getting near time to go when Emma asked him if he would like to come back to Drogheda and go to bed with her. She qualified this by saying that her son lived with her. The son would be out but would come back later, meaning that Mick would not be able to sleep in her bed. Mick couldn't believe his luck and not wishing to look a gift horse in the mouth, he agreed without condition. They hailed a taxi on Dawson Street and were soon dropped off at Connolly Station.

Mick had to get a ticket, but the queue was short. They were to take the Belfast Express. Emma had a note from her son telling her the times and which platform it departed from. There was a long queue, but soon the ticket collectors started letting people through and in no time, they were on the train. They found a carriage with adjacent seats and were soon joined by a middle-aged couple as the train filled up.

The train departed on time, and the couple across were discussing family matters. Mick guessed by their accent that they were from Dundalk or north of it. The train chugged out along the coast, passing one small station after another. Mick pointed out various landmarks such as Fairview Church away to the left, where his sister had been married many years before.

The train flew through Killester, Harmonstown and Kilbarrack. Mick thought of the days he used to take the Dart from Howth Junction to Blackrock. The train continued through Malahide and on to Lusk and Skerries with its two windmills. Mick remarked that it was over 20 years since he was on this train line. He marvelled at the new buildings; so many apartment blocks had sprung up in places like Donaghmede, Balbriggan and Donabate.

They glided along the coast of County Meath and talked about the annual horse races on the strand at Bellewstown. As they travelled northwards towards Drogheda, the Cooley Mountains came into view. Emma didn't seem to be familiar with the topography; she had only moved to County Louth in the recent past.

Away to the left, there was another mountain standing out on its own, and Mick surmised it was in Co Armagh. The man across heard him and joined in to confirm that it was Slieve Gullion and indeed it was in Armagh. Soon the man had Mick figured out as a Tyrone man and went on to tell Mick that Tyrone were lucky to have beaten Armagh in the All Ireland final five years before. He said Armagh had deserved to win. Mick looked at him but said nothing. He was thinking more of the romantic evening ahead.

As the train came near Drogheda, Emma and Mick left their seats ready to disembark and positioned themselves by the door. There was a small lad with a baseball cap and glasses standing there already. He had a large rucksack on his back.

The train came into Drogheda but didn't slow down. They knew there was something the matter when it sped straight through the station and over the high viaduct. Mick looked at Emma, and she looked at him and the little guy, who had a turn in his eye, looked at both of them.

The young lad then engaged Emma in conversation and informed her that this train often went on through Drogheda without halting. It was the Enterprise Express and that its first stop was Dundalk. Mick protested that he had a ticket stating he was going to Drogheda and shouldn't have been allowed through the barrier. Emma said hers was open for that line and could get on and off anywhere. They remained there and didn't go back to their seats. Mick didn't want to hear any more about Armagh's lack of footballing success. He thought it odd that this little guy was standing between carriages when there were plenty of seats inside. The wee man then volunteered to go off and find out why the train hadn't stopped in Drogheda. Shortly he was back to confirm that indeed the train didn't stop until it reached Dundalk.

After some time, the small man enquired of Emma if he might ask her a question. She laughed and said that he could. Emma was wearing a pair of white shoes with narrow pointed toes squared off at the end. He wanted to know if her feet were the same shape as the shoes! Emma just burst out laughing. Mick had suspected that the little man just wasn't firing on all cylinders, but this put the tin hat on it. Mick went inside and sat down, gesturing for Emma to follow as the next question might be unanswerable.

They got out in Dundalk and staff there informed them that there would be a train back to Drogheda in an hour. It would be going back empty and the driver would probably bring them along. They could go off into town and come back then. As they went up the steps at the exit, the little guy happened to be in front, and it was then they saw the long red scar down the back of his head. He had obviously had surgery. Emma felt sorry for him and Mick felt more than a little embarrassed. Emma castigated Mick for walking away from the man earlier. He had no reply.

The area around the station was pretty typical. There were the vacant lots where weeds grew and Mick visualised alcoholics and drug addicts congregating here late at night when everyone else was in bed. They passed a derelict pub which rejoiced in the title of The Railway Hotel. An old metal sign hung above the door advertising McArdles Ale, creaking as it oscillated gently in the breeze. They went into a pub called the Jockey and sat at the bar. Emma had more wine, and Mick had more tea. Emma was soon engaged in conversation with the lady behind the bar and Mick went to the men's room. When he returned, the ladies were involved in a conversation about some man who had given up cigarettes and someone who had passed away. He wasn't sure if it was the same man, but Emma then left to go outside for a smoke so Mick had to listen to the end of this story even though he didn't know the beginning and the lady gave no updates as it unfolded. He hadn't a notion what it was about but nodded furiously at what he| considered appropriate times. Emma came back, and soon they had to go again as it was now close to departure time.

Before they left, Emma mentioned condoms or the lack of them. Mick went to look in the toilets, but there were none. On their way back to the station, he decided to try a petrol station where he would be sure to find some. Emma went on ahead. But there were no condoms, and the young girl in there gave him a look that could wither a hippopotamus.

When Mick exited, he saw another petrol station almost adjacent to the first and thought he might have luck there. In he went, and it was a much bigger establishment. Again there was a young girl there, and again he got the evil eye and again drew a blank. It was now getting near departure time and he had to make haste back to the station where Emma was sitting in the waiting room. He then looked for condoms in the station toilets but to no avail. Emma told him not to be obsessive about it. Eventually, the train came and the guard introduced them to the driver who took the pair on board, and off they went on their merry way back to Drogheda where Emma's car was parked at the station.

This time there was no mistake and they were dropped off in Drogheda. They had just left the station when Mick spotted a garage and asked Emma to pull in. An Indian man was serving at the till and he was very happy to serve up a packet of condoms. Emma was surprised; she had said she couldn't imagine this place selling them at all. She was a regular customer and had never dreamt they sold condoms. Following their purchase, they drove on to Emma's place, which was out along the Boyne River. They drove under the big viaduct which they had crossed twice earlier.

Emma had to punch in her code to gain admittance and the big gates slowly unravelled. 'Oh no,' shrieked Emma as she reversed into her parking space. 'My son is here. His window is open. He is never here at this time, but today he is here. I have never known him to be here at this time of evening. What more can go wrong today?' They sat in the car, almost gutted, for what seemed like an age. A thousand mad thoughts crossed Mick's frustrated mind. He even thought of going home and then realised that idea wasn't a runner. So, after getting over their initial shock, they went in.

Emma had bought the apartment in poor shape and did it all up to her own taste. It was decorated impeccably and was her pride and joy. There was no sign of Emma's son. They had more wine and talked and then watched a football game. It was very relaxing. The son never appeared. He stayed in his room all the time, though Emma did claim to hear him rustling about once or twice.

Emma then ordered a Chinese takeaway and they ate that in the kitchen. There was more wine and also French coffee (coffee/brandy and sugar). Emma dimmed the lights and they snogged on the sofa. They soon gravitated onto the carpet and inevitably, they even tried out one of the condoms.

Mick was a bit apprehensive, but the whole exercise eventually came to a blissful conclusion, without distraction or interruption. Satisfied, a sudden tiredness descended on them after all their adventures. Off they went to bed together but in separate rooms.

Double Dutch

When Dutch Darcy arrived to see his friend Joe Doyle in Guangzhou he had a very brief initial introduction to the city. He spent a night and a day in the Cantonese capital during which time he did squeeze in a visit to a bar and a couple of restaurants. This, despite suffering from jet lag.

On the evening he arrived he had faded away about 11.00 pm and had to be helped to bed. The next day he and Doyle spent most of it in Zhujiang New Town where he was very impressed with the museum, the opera house and especially the library and its New Age design.

Doyle had been away from Ireland for some time and Dutch was keen to update him on events in their hometown. He got on to talking about his work in the community over the previous few years. He had set up a number of women's groups and joked that not a man in the town had had his shirt ironed in five years. He daren't appear in public as there was a bounty on him now!

Dutch was hardly 24 hours in town before Doyle and himself flew off to Ho Chi Minh City (HCMC). Dutch was really excited about the trip. He intended to make the most of getting away from his girlfriend and was making lots of plans to behave badly. Doyle had mixed feelings about all this as he had met the girlfriend, Fidelma, on several occasions. He also knew that she was blissfully unaware of the other Dutch of the hookers and good-time girls.

Dutch and Doyle arrived back in Guangzhou a week later. In HCMC a lot of Dutch's dreams apparently came true and he was in flying form on the way back. He was in reflective mood describing the lovely ladies he had encountered and reliving it all again. Of course he had further dreams which he hoped to realise in Guangzhou. He reminded Doyle of a kid in a sweetshop at these times. At other times of a dirty old man.

Back in Guangzhou after their week away they went first to Dutch's Hotel to drop off luggage. Dutch had stayed here for the one night before and loved it. It was modern and spacious with lots of facilities and all mod cons. Inevitably of course, he also had his eye on one of the receptionists.

They went on to Doyle's apartment before going out for dinner. Doyle was considering where Dutch might like to be taken. On the way out the door Doyle got a message from his friend Sharon. She was in trouble - locked out of her apartment. He finished by telling her to call later if she couldn't get back in. She could stay at his place if she was locked out.

Dutch reminded Doyle that he was to go to the bank to withdraw some money for him. He was nearly out of cash. So Doyle decided to go to ICBC. He would also be near Sharon's place if she called. Dutch expressed an interest in going to a street BBQ. So they headed that way and stopped at ICBC on the way. It took a while to get to the BBQ and they worked up a good appetite en route. When they got there they took a table, ordered food and beer and sat down. Dutch found it uncomfortable to sit on the low stool. He had hurt his back crawling through the Vietcong tunnels in Vietnam. Dutch was greatly impressed by the Chinese BBQ. The whole operation began nightly about 10.30 when the police went home. The team of barbecuers arrived on their little three-wheeled truck complete with all the food, a gas

BBQ, plates, cutlery, folding tables and small plastic stacking stools. They also provided tissues and chopsticks.

As soon as they arrived, the women put on their aprons, got the BBQ going and set out the tables and stools along the pavement. One lady cooked and another took orders and served the tables. They were always very busy. There must have been about 20 tables going.

Sharon texted to say that she still couldn't access her apartment and Doyle texted back to tell her where they were. She said she was coming. The food and Sharon eventually arrived together.

First they had lamb on skewers. Then they had more lamb. Then a big flat fish came followed by eggplant. They had skewered chicken wings, more lamb, and then BBQ chives which came on a kind of rack. There were all sorts of meat, fish and vegetables available and the only downside was the smell of gas and cooking oil. But they got over that and there was a great atmosphere abroad. All the people passing by were stopping to look, including many foreigners. Sharon didn't eat anything initially, but after a while, she did have some chicken wings and vegetables. They ordered another consignment of Pearl River Beer. Dutch really enjoyed the BBQ, gradually forgot about his backache and continually rubbed his belly in between ogling Sharon.

After they finished eating, Doyle asked Sharon if she minded walking back via Dutch's hotel. She said she had little alternative, so they headed in that direction. They encountered many tarts on the way. One lady followed them for a bit but dropped off when neither man showed any interest. Doyle and Sharon saw Dutch safely to the door of his hotel.

Doyle and Sharon went on back to Doyle's apartment. He made tea, gave her a bar of chocolate and suggested she could sleep on the couch. He brought her out a blanket, pillow, t-shirt and shorts. After changing she settled down in her makeshift bed. Doyle got into his own bed. Sharon kept talking over to him for a long time. It was mostly about her relationships, but she also mentioned Dutch and wasn't particularly enamoured by him. Dutch had made some inappropriate remarks which she didn't take kindly to. Doyle listened but said nothing and soon drifted off to sleep.

In the morning, Sharon was gone by the time Doyle arose from his slumbers. He had breakfast and went for a long walk. In the evening, he met Dutch and they went to a Dimsum restaurant. Some of Doyle's Chinese students also attended and they stayed there for two hours. Dutch really enjoyed the food once again. He was greatly impressed by the wide variety of dishes.

They followed this up with coffee. About 11 o'clock the students said they would go home. Before leaving, they talked about meeting the following Monday night when Dutch returned from a trip to Shanghai. He was off to visit his daughter who was teaching there.

The next day, Dutch arrived at Doyle's apartment where he arranged his belongings in various suitcases in readiness for his trip. While Dutch was packing, Doyle took a shower and then made tea. They went to a restaurant for dinner, had an after dinner walk and ended up in a Turkish coffee shop.

The cafe was busy but they found a table and ordered coffee. The eagle-eyed Dutch was surveying all the ladies, many of them foreigners. However, a Chinese girl really grabbed his attention. He was very excited. Doyle couldn't see the girl as she was behind him but he didn't need to, such was the detailed description Dutch provided along with a running commentary on her every move.

Dutch went to the toilet, but when he returned, he could no longer see the girl. She seemed to have disappeared into thin air. He was very agitated and kept looking round to see where she had gone. They lingered there for some time while Dutch pined for the lady's return. But it was not to be. When Dutch finally accepted that the girl had gone they left the coffee shop. They had talked about moving on to a bar, but Dutch suddenly became tired and didn't want to go. He went home. Doyle knew he was sulking.

On Monday morning, Doyle got up early, went walking around Luhu Lake, had a look in the art museum and then met Dutch in Starbucks; he seemed to be on an even keel. After coffee they went shopping. Dutch bought ten scarves and three keyrings. He was delighted with his purchases.

Doyle had promised to bring Dutch to a big market, but now Dutch had a change of mood and wanted to go straight to his hotel. Doyle's first reaction was disappointment, but it was soon followed by relief. He decided to go home and get a rest from Guangzhou, the world and the double Dutch man.

That evening after dinner, Doyle said he would bring Dutch to Tianhe, the new city centre and business district of Guangzhou. It had many new developments, including skyscrapers, a sports stadium and huge shopping malls.

They had a walk around the area, and Doyle thought Dutch would be impressed by the illuminated towers. But when they got there, Dutch seemed disinterested. His mind was elsewhere, and Doyle sensed him getting edgy. He said he wanted to find a cafe or bar. They passed several coffee shops, tea shops and wine bars but Dutch didn't like the look of any of them. Doyle asked if he wanted to go elsewhere.

Soon it became obvious what was up. Dutch wanted to go back to the Turkish coffee shop they were in the previous night; the place where he had seen that pretty girl. Again he described the young lady in great detail right down to her eyes, her hair, her makeup, her nails, her shoes, her mannerisms and how she carried herself. He seemed to have this idea that she would be there again.

They walked on for a bit but nothing was suitable for the lovestruck Dutch. He demanded they go to the metro. They were now walking in an unfamiliar area but Doyle figured there would be a metro station nearby; there always was.

Dutch still wasn't happy. When they didn't find a metro station immediately he announced that he would take a taxi. Doyle had had enough of his moods and didn't protest. Although it remained unsaid, he was pretty sure that Dutch was on his way to the Turkish Coffee Shop.

Doyle soon found a metro station and travelled home alone. It did take longer but he didn't have to listen to fantasies about a mysterious lady who was in a cafe last night and might be there again tonight.

Dutch wasn't seen again until he returned from Shanghai a week later. Before he left, Doyle's patience had been wearing thin and he was glad of a break from Dutch and the sulks and tantrums. Perhaps some time spent with his daughter would help Dutch to unwind.   There was a news blackout during this period. Doyle was relieved.

Dutch returned on the following Monday, and in the evening Doyle had arranged for them to go to dinner with the Chinese students and three western friends, Terry, Jackie and Amanda. Later they all went to the Vincent Bar and spent a few hours there. When the other people had departed, Dutch wanted Doyle to bring him to the Cave Bar. He had heard so much about it.

The Cave Bar, as the name suggested, was in a cellar and was a dark dimly lit establishment. It was a late-night haunt frequented by businessmen particularly from the Middle East and Africa.

There were always a few policemen lurking around the entrance and to gain admittance one also had to pass two burly security men. Inside, the bar was in the middle of the room with benches along the wall all the way round. There was a row of stools right around the bar. Inside the bar was a platform on which scantily-clad ladies took turns to gyrate and even dance.

Off to the side of the main bar was another smaller room. This room had a big cage in which ladies also performed for the assembled multitudes. The cage was probably to protect the girls from over-eager punters. Doyle loved watching all this. It wasn't so much the girls themselves but the Arab onlookers, drunk as skunks and with their eyes almost popping out of their heads.

As they arrived at The Cave there was a commotion going on at the bottom of the stairs, but that was nothing unusual and they headed on down anyway. A couple of drunk men were being led out by friends and accomplices.

It was bedlam in there. The place was in semi-darkness and shrouded in smoke. The multinational patrons were totally engrossed and the music was very loud. Ladies danced half-naked on top of tables, on the bar and in the cage. Little gangs of hookers could be seen here and there eyeing up prospective customers. It would have given any spectator a sore neck trying to take it all in.

As soon as Dutch sat down, a tall lady jumped up on his knee and started feeling around him, hugging him and nibbling at his ears. Dutch was revelling in it. Meanwhile, another tart was sitting at the corner of the bar beaming at him.

Dutch was now sweating and his tongue almost hanging out. Family man Dutch was very far away. Doyle, of course, realised there would eventually be a price to pay if this reached its conclusion. Luckily Dutch's attention wandered after a while and he moved on to the next group of ladies.

A few hookers came around Doyle too, but when he demanded money from them they cleared off. Many of them had met him before and knew how he would react to their attentions. One of them told Dutch that Doyle was "a bad man and didn't understand that she had to work." Doyle did have a chat with the cleaning lady who he was sure was the only female in there not looking for business of one sort or another.

Dutch was having the time of his life. He spent the night chatting to an endless number of pole dancers, lap dancers, limbo dancers, hookers, tarts and assorted hangers-on. He also got hit on by a male prostitute, which he definitely didn't relish, but which gave Doyle a great laugh. Later, when he described his experiences to others, Dutch said it felt like he had been through the Gates of Hell.

On Tuesday evening, Terry and Jackie invited Dutch out to dinner. They treated him. Later, Doyle met them all after he finished work. The ladies went off but said they might meet the men later. Doyle and Dutch went drinking. They weren't long in the bar when Doyle had a call from his friend Sharon and had to leave. Dutch said he would wait to see if Terry and Jackie returned.

Dutch was leaving for home early on Thursday and Doyle had arranged to meet on the Wednesday evening. Doyle also arranged for his colleague, Flann, to be there and to meet outside Doyle's workplace.

Flann arrived but Dutch was very late. Doyle had only an hour off between classes and now most of it was gone. He was miffed and let it be known.

Without warning, Dutch freaked out and threw his toys out of the pram. Doyle asked him to settle himself, but the harder he tried, the worse Dutch got. He started raving and accused Doyle of ruining his holiday. He then stormed off and ran down the stairs into the metro station as Doyle pleaded with him to come back.

Flann and Doyle ate dinner, but it was anti-climactic. Doyle wondered aloud what had gone on. Why had Dutch behaved like this, why could he take no criticism, why did he always had to have the last word, why was he so defensive and why couldn't he admit to mistakes? Flann was embarrassed and tried his best to be diplomatic. He couldn't say much; he had never met Dutch before.

Doyle thought back to his younger days in Ireland when Dutch and himself had had a big dispute over a girl and Dutch had behaved in the same way. They hadn't spoken for a long time afterwards. However, in recent years they had had a relatively amiable relationship despite Doyle's reservations about Dutch's treatment of his girlfriend.

Doyle didn't see himself as a great moralist, but it had troubled him how Dutch could be so sweet, so loving, so devoted and so caring to his lady but as soon as he went round the corner he took on a totally different persona. The family man morphed into a philanderer.

A few days later, Doyle met his friend Terry and she asked if Dutch had gone home. Doyle related the story of Dutch's dramatic departure. She expressed little surprise. She confided that she and Jackie hadn't been impressed with Dutch at all. In fact they couldn't wait to get away from him the last time.

Terry revealed she had had a bad feeling about Dutch from she first saw him and went on to describe him in very unflattering terms. She thought he was misogynistic, narcissistic, sleazy, creepy and extremely forward. Dutch had been all over Jackie the night they had gone to dinner. Neither of the ladies was impressed, especially as Dutch had had no encouragement.

A few months later, Doyle had a text message from a friend back in Ireland.

"Dutch and Fidelma got married last week."

Poor Fidelma, thought Doyle.

Gipsy Hill

It was around the turn of the millennium and Harry Walsh found himself living in London. His love life was at a low ebb and, as one does, he found himself placing an ad in the local free newspaper. He advertised as an Irishman new in town wanting to meet a lady for romance with the possibility of a long-term relationship.

There was some interest but nothing that had led anywhere until eventually he got a message from a lady who seemed very interested. Unfortunately, the battery in his phone gave up while she was in full flow.

He was out on the street at the time and a goodly distance from home. Curiosity overwhelmed him as he sought to reconnect with this mysterious lady. Needs must, they say, and so he retired to a McDonald's where he was able to recharge the handset as he feasted on the delights and surprises of a Big Mac and a Happy Meal.

When a suitable time had elapsed and he calculated that he had enough charge, he called again. On the first attempt, he had gathered the lady's name was Diane but she had wittered on so much about her life, her loves, her rows and her relations that she hadn't reached the part where she revealed her number before being cruelly and abruptly silenced.

Now he had to listen through this long speech again and hope that in the end she would cough up the magical eleven digits. Again, he heard about her love of this, that and the other, how many evening classes she attended, the colour of her hair (it was brown), her artistic temperament (she liked sewing) and a lot of the usual statistics of would-be romantic partners.

Eventually, she finished off with the phone number and gave him the option of calling if he felt he wanted to proceed. Harry went outside onto Tooting Broadway and was so excited he rang immediately without any thought or preparation. He began by telling his new friend where he was, the circumstances of being there, why he wasn't ringing from home and his very recent visit to the famous Scottish restaurant.

They then engaged in serious discussions on the night classes, her job and her life in general. It turned out she was from Bristol but had been in London for some years. She was a trained nurse and worked as a nanny for a rich family in North Kent. She talked quite a lot about this and about her previous employment which had ended a few months ago and how the kids were very bold, but she had loved them anyway. Harry thought that was very noble of her without actually putting it into words.

She went on to tell him about her interest in forensics and how she was studying in Clapham three nights a week. She really enjoyed her class and liked one of the male tutors but wasn't too keen on her female tutor who seemed distant, cold and always tired.

Diane originally thought she was the only person who didn't get on with this female tutor but was relieved to discover that several other students also had difficulty with this woman. She went into great detail about how this lady taught kids all day and was probably tired and offhand when it came to the night class. She said too that she had confided in her favourite male tutor about her dislike of this lady. The man hadn't reacted.

She kept ranging over a variety of topics and talked about

having been hurt in the past etc. She was just warming up on this topic when Harry saw his credit was running out. Before he ended the call, he asked if she was available on Saturday night.

He promised to ring again when he got home and he did. The phone call at home lasted over two hours. In the course of this conversation he heard more. She talked a lot about her drinking habits after first telling him that she wasn't supposed to drink or smoke because of a kidney condition. From what she told him she drank often and much. She prided herself on being able to obtain alcohol at any time of day or night and being able to persuade pub landlords to stay open just for her. She didn't change her habits either on visits home to Bristol. Her parents couldn't understand her coming home at 3.00 am rather than at 11.05 pm.

Diane went on to tell Harry about being in Norfolk camping at the New Year and having to come back when she became very ill with some kind of stomach infection. He was wondering about these tales of woe and how so many came to befall a single person.

She expanded on the night classes and described everyone in the class and where they all sat in the class. There was one blonde lady with green eyes who always asked stupid questions and a man with a limp who she felt sorry for. Then she talked about some of them whom she knew socially and who travelled with her in the car to the class. They were a foursome, two women and two men and sometimes they went drinking afterwards. There was no romance though. She did say she had feelings for one of the men but that was as far as it had gone so far. Harry didn't pursue this topic. Diane admitted to being a bit paranoid and seldom ventured out alone. She was deeply hurt from her last affair, which was a long and winding story. This man had been with her for several months. He had been married but left his wife and came to live with her.

Everything in that particular garden was very rosy, but then out of the blue her partner had left and gone back to his wife. What was even more bizarre was that he wasn't long back with his wife before he upped sticks and went off with a third party. It was a muddled story.

On one occasion, Diane had been taken to this man's house when the wife was on holiday and had noticed certain things in certain places in the bedroom wardrobe, which suggested he was sleeping with the wife when he had told Diane he wasn't. Harry wondered why she was in the bedroom of another person's house, never mind the wardrobe.

She then went on to describe how she went to church every Sunday "to embarrass the bastard." Her going there was very awkward for many people, especially as she would sit right up at the front. Harry wasn't following the story very carefully and was in a kind of daydream. That was until she revealed that her lover was the local Church of England vicar.

Next, he heard about the time she had been raped by someone she knew. She found it difficult to trust men and was only talking to Harry because he was Irish. She had been hurt many times in the past and was wary. She would only sleep with a man who wanted her for the rest of her life. Harry wondered how she could foresee that, but he decided it was best to keep his counsel.

During this conversation, a knock came to the door and she answered it. She had her button coded so she knew the caller's identity and so let in this friend, a man. He had a carry out for her and she temporarily abandoned her phone while she fetched a fork. Harry now heard a miaowing sound. Diane hadn't mentioned that she had a cat but the beast now started to cry for food. She shut it in the kitchen, but it could still be heard loud and clear. A conflict then arose between her and the friend over feeding the cat. The friend let the cat in again and started giving it chips. She maintained the cat had already been fed.

Harry was assured that Sylvester was usually quiet and that this, as yet unnamed, man teased him. The man accused her of being bad to the cat. She then accused the man of throwing a cup of tea over the cat four years ago from which the creature had a permanent scar and an open sore.

Harry had difficulty getting the lady off the phone. Before letting her go he had arranged to meet her at Gipsy Hill railway station the next evening. He was again left with much to ponder and he wondered if he was a glutton for punishment. But he couldn't stop himself.

This all happened at the time of the great monsoon of autumn 2000 and so he set off in a downpour for Gipsy Hill on that fateful Saturday evening not knowing quite what to expect. He got a tube to Balham and then took a train. The journey went smoothly and he arrived in Gipsy Hill about half an hour early. Predictably, Gipsy Hill station sits on the brow of a hill. It is a dull nondescript place at the best of times, but on a wet evening it is beyond depressing. It was still bucketing rain, but despite the circumstances Harry remained optimistic. He went into a chippie and bought two big sausages. He followed up by buying a packet of sweets and a drink from a corner shop. It was nearly eight, but there was no sign of Diane.

He retreated into the station, where at least there was shelter. He positioned himself near the entrance where he could look out for his honey date. From time to time, ladies would walk past but no one stopped. Harry suddenly realised he had no picture nor any means of recognising her if she did appear. He didn't mind and at this stage wasn't overly concerned. He always expected ladies to be late. Harry was approached by a homeless man who was very persistent. He had to get off the concourse to escape. He stood outside on the porch and the rain was coming down in rods. Eight o'clock came and went but the voice wasn't to be seen.

He still wasn't alarmed but at 8.30 there was a growing sense of unease and a cause for concern. A crowd of teenagers had gathered and were messing around in the station foyer. Harry was nervous. There was no one else around. Every time a woman walked past he wondered if that was her coming to have a look at him without revealing herself.

One strange lady arrived dressed only in striped pyjamas and a pair of pink carpet slippers. She could have been in her late thirties or early forties but she had seen better days. She was slightly stooped as she moved slowly along, her piercing eyes looking out from a gaunt and wrinkled face.

This lady peered at him and then stood for some time studying the train timetable before waddling back up the street in the rain. Harry had a feeling that might have been her. She did look at him knowingly. He didn't like the look of her so didn't say anything. But how could he know for sure?

At about 8.45, he decided to give up the ghost and went for the 9 o'clock train. The rain kept beating down mercilessly. He went down onto the platform, but no train came as he sat looking at the rain, looking at the people on the opposite platform and the procession of trains going the other way.

There was a group of French people, and one lad got out a Rod Stewart wig, put it on and sang Maggie May on the platform. There were two ladies sitting next to him. One had an Irish accent, but Harry made no attempt to strike up conversation. He stayed close to his thoughts. The rain leaked through the roof ... drip drip drip.

Eventually, the train came; it was an hour late. He embarked and sat there silently looking straight ahead; he was stunned. After some time had passed he stretched himself, sighed, looked around at his fellow passengers who he had suddenly become aware of. He began to laugh to himself. There was nothing else for it.

Did he deserve this? Should he have anticipated or expected

this outcome? Why didn't he see the red flags which had appeared all through his conversations with the lady? As Gipsy Hill faded into the distance, he concluded that he just didn't have the hindsight at the right time.

Mr Ben

There is something unique about fast food joints and the type of clientele they attract. No doubt they would proudly boast that their customers come from all sections of society. So it was one summer evening after work when a chilled out Larry O Connor popped into that great melting pot, the KFC on Tooting Broadway. Sometimes he liked to have a beer after class, but this time he had a hankering for a chicken meal and a Pepsi Cola.

O Connor had been teaching at the local adult education centre for several years and this evening he felt good after a session with his multinational band of students. He was a quiet bespectacled unassuming bachelor, small in stature and in his mid-forties, who had dedicated most of his life to helping others through his work as a literacy tutor.

There was but a scattering of people inside the red-tinted world and O Connor had the rare luxury of a table to himself. Once he had eaten a few fries, tasted the chicken and had a sip of his cola he stopped to draw breath and soak up some atmosphere, even ambience. To his left was a noisy family group who were caught up in their own world of nuggets, wings and ketchup. To his right sat a black lady all by herself, drinking coffee from a red paper cup. Their eyes met briefly, O Connor smiled and she smiled back.

For some reason, this lady took O Connor's interest, and he

found himself involuntarily studying her whilst trying not to stare and not be caught looking. She was probably about 55, taller than himself and on the plump side of medium. She was wearing a brown raincoat and what appeared to be a flowery dress underneath. There was a grey furrow down her hair, parting suggesting that a visit to the hairdresser would soon be on the agenda. She looked nervous and was constantly scanning the restaurant in a distracted, restless way.

It wasn't long before she addressed O Connor, "I know you."

This startled O Connor. His glasses almost hopped off his nose. He had sensed that there was something about her, but he wasn't aware that he actually knew her.

"Is that so? How do I know you?"

She smiled. "You may not know me, but I know you, Mr Larry. My name is Miriam. I attend evening classes at your school. You teach English, don't you?"

"I do indeed," replied the recovering O Connor as he tried to refocus on the Sanders diet.

After he had partaken of some more fries and chicken washed down with cola, O Connor paused again. The lady noticed that he had stopped eating and leaned over to show him something she had written on a brown paper KFC bag.

"Can you check the grammar and spelling for me?" she asked.

O Connor checked the text and assured her that it was fine. It said, "People buy things which are not always useful." There was a word crossed out as well which he couldn't make out. She kept talking, but O Connor couldn't understand all she was saying. She saw that he wasn't familiar with her accent and inched closer as she talked. When she smiled, she lit up and almost looked pretty.

This piece of writing was intriguing O Connor as he tried to tease out the connection to the lady before him. Miriam must have just written it but he couldn't gauge what it referred to. Maybe it wasn't even referring to her! Perhaps it was a general philosophical observation! Had she seen or heard this expression somewhere, been taken by the words and copied them?

O Connor was aware that people do spend money on unnecessary things and in his time he ruefully remembered having been guilty of the practice himself. Items like Lotto tickets, exercise clothing, detoxes, air fresheners, multivitamins, power tools, suede shoes, foreign holidays, takeaway food and designer brands all came to mind.

However, O Connor wasn't sure whether it was any of the aforementioned items she was referring to. Of course, a lady could be referring to scented trash bags, cookbooks, baby shoes, fancy underwear, body lotions, manicures or even pedicures.

He took a good long look at her now. She didn't appear to be someone who lived in a big house or owned a Rolls Royce. However, there was no way of knowing if she spent a lot of money on dog groomers. Did her kitchen contain garlic peelers, melon wedgers, banana slicers, asparagus peelers, peach pitters, avocado cutters, onion dicers or other seldom-used items? O Connor couldn't tell!

Because he was lacking in knowledge of the specifics, O Connor thought it wiser to offer some very general advice re keeping away from temptation, avoiding retail seduction, taking an inventory and instituting a 24-hour hold policy. He even quoted one Edward Norton. "We buy things we don't need with money we don't have to impress people we don't like."

He kept eating intermittently and each time he paused she would speak. She kept pointing to the piece of text and trying to explain its significance. O Connor was embarrassed as he prided himself on being a good listener. Eventually, an embarrassed O Connor realised that she had just come from a class where they had been discussing English proverbs. She wanted to practice!

When she saw that O Connor now understood she relaxed and went on to tell him that she was from Ghana but had been domiciled in England for a number of years. She then asked where he was from.

He was about to reply that he was from Ireland, but before he could get the words out she asked if he was English. When she heard he was Irish she wanted to know if he was from the north or the south. After he told her that he was from Fermanagh her eyes lit up and she revealed that she had a lover from those parts, a place called Boho.

O Connor made some general enquiries about this boyfriend and asked if he was here with her in London. She said that at present he was far away but didn't give any further details. He then inquired if she would be reunited with him in the near future. Miriam didn't reply to that but just kept on talking and occasionally would burst out laughing. It was a kind of unnatural belly laugh. Eventually, she declared that she loved this man, but "Only God knows when I will see him again."

Meanwhile, another black girl sat down nearby. She was in her twenties, well dressed, slim and pretty with it. O Connor could smell a fruity perfume and with her pink lipstick and red high heels she was certainly attractive. She had been listening in to the conversation whilst attending to her drumsticks, fries and chicken tenders.

This girl had been giggling as she listened to the love story. Miriam had noticed this, which only served to embolden her. She continued talking about her lover and also brought her own husband into the conversation, describing him as a good man but one she didn't love.

Her lover was named Mr Benjamin, Mr Ben for short. Miriam spoke about him in the most glowing terms, but such was the lengthy list of superlatives, O Connor wondered if this Mr Ben had ever been anything but a dream. Then she dropped her bombshell. Mr Ben had been dead for 20 years and she had left her husband immediately after hearing the news, never to return. At the time, her husband questioned why she was leaving the house dressed in black and so she explained to him that she was going to a wake. O Connor exchanged glances with the second lady. This story was becoming increasingly bizarre and the teller was now becoming excited and also agitated.

Miriam then talked about her relationship with Mr Ben's wife, Abigail. She had been a frequent visitor to their house when Mr Ben was alive. On one occasion Mr Ben had brought Miriam into his bedroom but she had declined to get into bed as the wife was in the house at the time.

Miriam then claimed that she and the wife had an understanding. As evidence, she pointed out how well she had been received at the wake. On arrival, she had been brought into the parlour with the VIP mourners and had been treated to food and drink. Miriam had then been invited to stay over for the funeral. In fact, she remained there for the duration of the wake and attended the funeral in the company of Mr Ben's wife. After the funeral Mrs Ben asked her if she wanted to come and live with her and she accepted. The two of them had been living happily together ever since.

Following all these revelations, the younger lady couldn't resist joining the conversation. She introduced herself as Abebi from Nigeria and she began questioning Miriam about this relationship with Mr Ben. "Did you not feel guilty at the time, especially that you also knew his wife?"

Miriam didn't reply.

"Was it right and proper to be involved with a married man?" she persisted.

Even a dead married man? thought O Connor!

Miriam wasn't going to take this lying down for long and, fresh from her class on proverbs, quoted "All's fair in love and war." She backed up her assertion by introducing the ancient prophet Abraham, of Bible and Koran fame, who had four wives. She knew all their names and also mentioned that Abraham had fifteen children. O Connor was now temporarily sidelined but struggled to keep his composure as he listened to the conflicting arguments.

The adulterer went on to back up her assertions with a reference to King Solomon, who reputedly had 700 wives with 300 concubines thrown in for good measure. She pointed out too that he was still a very popular man in Ghana 3,000 years later. In fact there was even a football team in the city of Nkawkaw named after him.

"How come you can't put this man behind you after 20 years?" queried Abebi.

Miriam was ready for her again and once more her recent English class stood to her.

"Absence makes the heart grow fonder," she countered.

Abebi then quoted Thomas Paine, "Divided love is never happy."

Miriam was having none of it and immediately came back with, "Grief divided is made lighter." And so it went on. No matter what was said, it made not a whit of difference to Miriam. The love affair with Mr Ben couldn't be derailed so easily and indeed it looked set to continue for another twenty years at least, with or without his presence. Eventually, Abebi gave up, shrugged her shoulders, gathered up her belongings, bade both of them farewell and left. Miriam appeared to be on the verge of crying.

O Connor had long finished the chips, chicken and coke and now found himself sitting staring into the depths of an empty cardboard box. He looked up to see two sad sobbing brown eyes as Miriam muttered,

"Mr Ben."

A mixed bag of unanswered questions swirled around in Larry O Connor's head as he prepared to depart the "Finger-lickin' good" world of the fake colonel. Did Mr Ben ever exist? Was he a fake too? How did Miriam end up being so friendly with the wife?

Just as O Connor got up to go, curiosity got the better of him and he enquired of Miriam how she and Mrs Ben were able to get on so well together despite being such great love rivals.

Miriam looked steadily at O Connor and in a deadpan kind of way drawled, "Abigail is my sister." She coolly regarded the enlightened but motionless O Connor, leaned back and added, "As you well know Mr Larry, blood is thicker than water."

Sharon and the Snapper

J oe Doyle had been in Guangzhou about a year when he first
encountered Sharon. They had been chatting online for a
time before they met. Their first face to face meeting was
outside the Guangzhou Friendship Store in Taojin.

Sharon was late and then when she did arrive they couldn't
decide where to go. After some deliberation and discussion they
set off for the Edge, a nearby bar. They had drinks and listened to
a jazz band. It was a very laidback kind of depot, but Sharon was
restless and soon wanted to move.

The next port of call was the Haagen-Dazs ice cream parlour
and there they had two bowls of ice cream, one each. All the
waitresses were dressed in kilts, tartan and Tam o' Shanters. Clearly
as Scottish as McDonald's. To Doyle it was an odd environment.
It was packed with people of various nationalities including
Chinese, Indians, Arabs and South Americans. To them it
probably wasn't in the least bit odd. The ice cream was very good
despite the price being exorbitant. They stayed there until midnight
when they were asked to leave. It was time for the shop to close.

When they got outside, Sharon asked Doyle if he would like to
go walking. It was late, but he was off the next morning so away
they went. They walked towards Baiyun Mountain and came on a
big night market with crowds of people milling around and a lot
of barbecuing going on. The mixed aromas of meat, vegetables,

gas and burning oil was strong and all pervasive. Many of the BBQs were run by Muslims so there was no pork on the menu. Those with an aversion to eating dog would also have been quite safe as the sons of the prophet regard dogs as unclean as pigs. There was skewered mutton, chicken pieces, chicken wings, chicken feet, beef, several kinds of fish, octopus, eggplant, greens and corn on the cob. Several types of shellfish were being cooked in their shells.

They walked up a very quiet street on their way to a lake which Sharon was familiar with. It commenced to rain, but luckily, Doyle had with him a recently bought golf umbrella which was big enough for the two of them. Just as the rain started to come down, Denis, Doyle's colleague, texted him wanting to know where he was, who he was with and what was going on. Doyle thought the best reply was to put Denis on to Sharon and so Denis heard the whole story direct from the horse's mouth. Sharon and Doyle ended up walking right round the bigger than expected lake and it took about two hours. There was decking all the way around and the walkway was illuminated. Although the lakeside restaurants were closed there were still plenty of people around.

On the way back, they decided to stop at the BBQ and began modestly with a lamb kebab each. They followed that up with chicken and then beer. Sharon was enjoying listening to Doyle reading a string of very suggestive texts frm Denis. Then they walked back to the Friendship Store at about 2.30 am. Sharon suggested they go home from there, each by their separate ways. But they didn't. They stood there talking until 5.30 am. Sometimes it rained and they put up the umbrella. Then it would stop. Later on it came on very heavy which necessitated Sharon getting out her umbrella as well.

While they had been walking, Sharon wanted to know all about Doyle, which was hardly unusual for a lady. She was enquiring about his family, his work history and last but not least his history with ladies. She was especially interested in ladies he had known during his time in China. He provided a potted and much-edited synopsis with some detail on Mandy and Susan, the two he remembered most about.

Then when they stopped, the focus shifted to her love life and remained there for the remaining time they spent together. The central figure in this saga was Erik, a German photographer.

Sharon claimed to have known this character for years. Over that period, every time he came to Guangzhou, he would ring her and they would usually have dinner together. He was a very good friend, resided in Hong Kong but frequently travelled into mainland China. He had told her he was divorced with one son. He and Sharon got on very well and he always "behaved like a gentleman." He sounded like someone's ideal man, he never shouted nor did he ever anger.

Their relationship was purely platonic over this long period of time. She had boyfriends and he had girlfriends, but that was never discussed as it was of no concern given they were only friends.

Then, over the last while, things had changed. The lensman started sending her messages when he was absent telling her that he really missed her, couldn't live without her and wanted them to have a relationship. Sharon said that she then reacted and started to develop similar feelings for him.

In the end, at some recent point, they were together and she admitted to having enticed him into bed. Of course she didn't go into the details of this amorous encounter, but it was a very deep and moving experience for her, and apparently for him too.

The next morning he rushed off and she didn't hear from him again that day. She was upset and angry. On the following day, she messaged him and communicated her disquiet. He then apologized for whatever unknown sin he had committed and promised he would speak to her about 'things' next time.

There followed a next time, a Round 2, and the same thing happened again. Off he went in the morning without expressing any feelings or talking about the things she wanted to talk about. Following the second encounter the relationship had broken down and now she didn't talk to him at all. She was very confused as to what had happened and what she had done, what he had done, how it could have been different, why men are like this, how this, how that, how the other?

Doyle tried to tell her that this kind of stuff happens and she wasn't the first person to have suffered this sort of behaviour from a man. He ventured the opinion that perhaps some people found it difficult to express themselves emotionally. "Wasn't he a German? That was their nature. They don't do emotion." This upset her. She repeated her mantra that he was a true gentleman, that he never got cross or raised his voice and was always very courteous and kind.

Doyle tried to tell her that Erik may well have been all these things, but that didn't mean that he was 'caring.' He ventured the opinion that being caring and in tune with his emotions was another matter entirely and didn't automatically follow from being gentle and kind. She couldn't swallow this new hypothesis at all and at times was almost getting aggressive with Doyle.

The golf umbrella had now broken with all the upping and downing. The Velcro on the strap wasn't sticking. Doyle worked at it but without success. It would entail a visit to the umbrella repairman the next day. The discussion kept going round and round. Sharon wasn't hearing what Doyle was saying and he wasn't hearing what she was saying. Neither was reading between the lines. He told her that it wasn't fair asking him to solve the problem of her last boyfriend at a time when he himself was hoping to develop a relationship with her. He really wasn't the person to be dispassionate or neutral on this matter. Sharon thought she needed to learn from her experience. Doyle tried to tell her that, in his opinion, there was no lesson to be learned and that a lot of these relationship matters defied logic. Something happened at some point in her or Eric's unconscious mind that changed things but which couldn't be voiced. "You start off with a clean sheet every time you meet someone and you hope it works out. If things go wrong it's too bad; you have to roll with the punches; you have to adjust to the rough and tumble," Doyle offered.

Doyle's message was still not being received. She kept going back to the same thing; Erik was such a kind man, a gentleman to boot. Therefore it followed that he had to be 'caring'. Was it that Doyle's counselling skills were letting him down again? Was his message not strong enough? Was it unclear? Was it the right message for her at that time?

They were making no headway so they decided finally to go home. Doyle was only giving an opinion and it was none of his business anyway. Before they parted he asked if she wanted him to go home with her. She gave him a long hard look but didn't answer. He didn't press her!!!

On his way home, Doyle was asking himself "Have I caught another Tartar?" He also asked himself if he should cut his stick and get out of this situation while the going was good or did he want to hear this litany of rhetorical questions repeated over and over, generating even more questions which could never be answered in a way that was satisfactory to her?

Doyle forgot about it as soon as he fell asleep, but two days later found himself back with Sharon again, this time in The Lemon House, a Thai restaurant. It was fairly late. She ordered some food but didn't like it. She said the meat wasn't cooked very well. She asked for it to be reheated but it still didn't please her. She paid and then they left there and went to McDonald's where she wanted a McFlurry. They sat in McDonald's for about 20 minutes. There was a legless beggar lying sleeping in one chair by the window. At the back of the shop a solitary lady was sitting looking into space with an empty beer bottle in front of her. She was dozing on and off, sometimes waking up with a start, looking all around her and then slumping back in her seat. There were a few other assorted characters mostly young couples. One pair were sitting talking and occasionally, she would hit him a box, as Chinese girlfriends do.

After a while they left and went to Costa Coffee. Doyle had tea and Sharon had a mug of water. She was very edgy and started to get argumentative. She was greatly bothered by the fact that Doyle had suggested going to her house the previous time. She accused him of taking her for a hooker and stormed off. That was that. He texted her later, but she didn't reply.

Next day, Denis texted to tell Doyle that Sharon had contacted him. Doyle met him later and Denis revealed Sharon had been complaining to him about Doyle and alleged that Doyle had called her a hooker. Denis just told her he couldn't comment as it was none of his business. He thought she was slightly mad. At that time Doyle thought he would hear no more of her.

Several weeks passed. Then one evening Doyle was sitting at home minding his own business and listening to a football match on the radio when the phone rang. It was Sharon. She said she was near his house and wanted to meet. She was on her way to Starbucks.

Doyle went to Starbucks and then realised he didn't remember what she looked like. He looked around downstairs but there were no likely females there. Upstairs he saw one lady sitting alone but he wasn't sure if it was her and didn't recognise her so he stayed away from her. He waited. After some time he rang and Sharon picked up. She told him she was at the front door. Doyle went downstairs again and looked around. He could see nobody near the door, least of all a single lady. Then he put his head outside and next thing Sharon was beside him. She had a lad with her. This boy she had with her was a strange-looking being. Doyle thought he resembled some cartoon character, possibly Shrek. He was of average height and build but had no neck as such. On his shoulders sat a huge round head with two protruding red ears. He spoke little but wore a constant grin.

Doyle remembered Sharon now that he had seen her. She was very pale with freckles. He asked what she had been up to and she replied 'living'. He asked again as to what she had been doing this evening and she divulged that she and her friend had been to a restaurant. Shrek nodded furiously in agreement.

Sharon said that her friend wanted to improve his English. She gave Doyle a brief rundown on the boy and his career to date. All the while he kept smiling and nodding like one of those car window dogs. The thought crossed Doyle's mind that the whole purpose of the meeting was to get a free English lesson. He was very tired and after a decent amount of time had elapsed he left them there sipping their iced teas and went home.

Again Doyle put Sharon out of his mind until about a week later he was out walking, just wandering along in a daydream, when who should he bump into but Sharon. She asked him where he was going. He said nowhere in particular and she suggested they go for a walk and she would show him a few bars nearby which she thought he might like to visit sometime. So they walked around and she showed him a few places. She told him that she had been spending a lot of time in her hometown as her father had been ill. There was no mention of the German or Shrek.

After that, Doyle didn't hear from her for another six weeks until he got a call one night about 11.00 pm. She was in a nearby McDonald's and invited him to come down. When he arrived,

Sharon, as was her wont, wanted to walk. He asked her about her father. He had had a stroke, but now he was improving. The family lived in Hunan, the next province to Guangdong. Her mother was also poorly with what sounded like sciatica, an uncle had just died from colon cancer and an aunt was in hospital. All in all a pretty stressful time of it if she was to be believed.

They followed a familiar route, under the railway bridge, up the hill and left at the top. Doyle knew they were off to the BBQ. Lamb kebabs, chicken kebabs, vegetables and beer were selected from the menu. They sat down and waited to be served. Cars pulled up, people collected food and off they went again. Small trucks pulled up and were left parked halfway out on the eight-lane highway while the occupants had a BBQ. There were several BBQs along the street and some more down an alleyway nearby. Their food came incrementally and while they waited they ordered more beer.

After they finished the BBQ, they went back down the hill. They thought they might try some noodles, but as they approached the noodle restaurant Sharon started cursing. It was closed. So they walked on. They were not to be denied and soon found another noodle bar where they ordered noodles with beef and dumplings. After they ate, Sharon said she was tired and wanted to go home.

Relations between them had stabilised somewhat and the following week they decided to go for dinner to a Cantonese restaurant. Sharon arrived, wearing a white dress and looked very well, angelic even. Doyle enquired about her father and she revealed that he was now able to walk about a little but his speech was badly affected. She was worried about him, especially as the mother was also partially incapacitated.

After they left the restaurant, Sharon of course wanted to go for a walk. Although she loved walking she only ever wore a pair of flip flops. On this route they passed a lot of Middle Eastern stores, coffee shops and even a wine shop or two. Sharon decided she wanted to change direction and show Doyle another place. Here there were numerous cafes, restaurants and shops, again with a strong Arabic flavour.

She was constantly talking as she walked. She mentioned Doyle's son and told him that he wasn't giving Doyle junior enough money. She said Doyle was too fat, that he ate too much, that he ate too fast and all those familiar observations that many others had made over the course of Doyle's time on the planet. Then she gave him her opinions on love and romance. She said she didn't need anyone to tell her they loved her continually or to keep asking her if she loved them.

They walked on and ended up at Doyle's local Starbucks. They had drinks and talked for nearly an hour. There was an odd-looking lady sitting near them. She had her hair up in a bun, was wearing glasses and kept grinning at Doyle like a Cheshire Cat. He didn't recognise this person, but she was obviously on the lookout for a victim (he was to encounter this character again later). Sharon and Doyle then went off home, she going her way and he his.

Around this time they continued to meet regularly. Sharon was always active late at night and one night it was after midnight when she called to ask Doyle out to eat. They walked to Xiaobei and had noodles in what was reputedly one of the top noodle restaurants in Guangzhou.

There weren't many people in it. One girl was inside cooking. There were two other members of staff, a girl sitting at the table next to them texting on her mobile and another girl on a laptop at another table, smoking like a train and totally focused on an online game. Four men, including the owner, sat at a table near the door, talking and smoking. A delivery man brought in bags of BBQ food to the girl on the laptop and the texter. It was a bit ironic that they didn't eat their own food.

There had been no mention of the German paparazzo for a long time, but that night as they walked, Sharon began to talk about him again. He still remained a preoccupation. He was perplexing her. He hadn't been heard of for months but had texted her the previous day.

According to her, he had texted, she had replied, but then he didn't answer her. She wanted to know why. She couldn't understand. Doyle ventured the opinion that he was probably playing mind games. She kept asking Doyle why he would do that. Doyle explained that there was no reason at all. Maybe he was mad, he speculated!

"What do you mean by mad?" she asked.

Doyle explained that the guy might be crazy in some way. Then she stated that he was very normal and she had known him for a long time. Deja vu?

Doyle asked her if she wanted to see this guy. Did she want to bring him back into her life? Did she want to have sex with him again? She replied that she was single and could have sex with whoever she wanted. She kept wanting to know why this man was behaving like this. More deja vu?

Once again, this conversation kept going round in circles. Doyle suggested that if the man was genuinely interested in her he would make a bigger effort to communicate. She mentioned at one point that previously when they were just friends, he invariably rang at 9.00 pm. That disconcerted her. Doyle asked if he was married. She didn't know. She said she had never been to his house although she had been invited.

Doyle kept telling her to forget this man as there was nothing to be gained from thinking about it. He tried to explain the parable of Brer Rabbit and the Tar-Baby, which may or may not have been inappropriate. She didn't want to listen to that, and then she went on the offensive, telling him that he wasn't advising her properly.

She said Doyle didn't know this man. Doyle admitted that he didn't know this particular man but that he had heard the same or a very similar story from many other ladies and the men were always playing the same game. She was having none of that and began to defend the German more and more.

Next thing, she accused Doyle of only being interested in getting her into bed. She was probably partially right. By this time, they were back to where they had first met. Doyle said he was going home and asked her if she wanted to come. Of course this greatly annoyed her to the point that Doyle was able to escape quickly without getting into another rigmarole.

When Doyle and Sharon disagreed strongly about the German, there was always a long interlude until the next encounter. This time it ended one night when she texted to tell him that she was locked out. At that moment, Doyle was with his Irish friend Dutch who was visiting China. He told her to call later and that if she couldn't get in she could stay at his house.

Dutch and Doyle went to a BBQ and Doyle texted Sharon to tell her where they were. She said she was coming. When they finished eating Sharon accompanied Doyle and Dutch back to Dutch's hotel as the new arrival had no sense of where he was.

They did manage to get Dutch home safely, for once, and then walked to Doyle's apartment. Doyle made tea, gave Sharon some chocolate to eat and made up a bed for her on the couch. He provided her with a pair of shorts and a t-shirt. She changed and settled down on the couch. Doyle put on some music for her before he went to his own bed.

Sharon talked for a long time about her relationships and dealings with men. A classmate of hers had tried to rape her a few weeks ago when she went to visit her father. This guy was a policeman and wanted her to have a baby for him. He had a daughter already with his wife but wanted a son.

Doyle heard about another married classmate who had called her after not hearing from him for years. He was in Guangzhou for the weekend and suggested meeting up. He too wanted sex and tried to force himself on her.

Then she told Doyle about an American she had had a relationship with. He must have been someone she met online and at a time before the snapper had appeared. She described how the Yank had been such a gentleman and called her every day and was always asking her how she was and really cared about her. *Par for the course,* thought Doyle!!!!

This American had come to China to visit her. It was his first visit to the country but he had then visited regularly every few months. He had shown great devotion, professed his undying love, was very good-looking, fit and visited the gym regularly. He had worked for an airline but wasn't a pilot. Doyle asked her why she didn't marry him and she said he married someone else – a Vietnamese woman he had met in America. But there was no explanation how that had come about.

Then she went back to the Swedish guy, Erik (Doyle had always thought he was German, but now she insisted he was a Swede). Doyle had heard much about him of course over the last few months but now he had a feeling she was coming round to the possibility that Erik was a weirdo and an insincerista. They ate some more chocolate on and off and gradually went to sleep. There may have been further stories, but Doyle missed them as he migrated to the Land of Nod.

They met again a few nights later and Sharon gave Doyle a carrier bag with two packets of tea and a set of little teacups inside. They decided to go to a bar and then on to the Porridge Restaurant which was humming as usual and where they had noodles. Then they went to McDonald's for ice cream and sat until after 1.00 am.

Sharon was talking again about the husbands of all her female classmates. From what Doyle could make out, Sharon had little confidence in men; who could blame her? She was also worried about the man who recently fixed her door after she was locked out, in case he could gain access to her apartment.

She spoke of a discussion with a female friend about their common male school friend who had met Sharon recently and suggested she go to bed with him despite the fact that he was married. This lady had then gone on to confide in Sharon about her own husband's infidelity. Sharon lamented the infidelity of the husbands of all her friends.

Doyle was meeting Sharon regularly again around this time and the next occasion they met, Sharon invited Doyle to McDonald's to eat burgers. They talked a while, or rather she talked a while. Firstly she berated him for his attitude towards the African drug dealers who were swarming around the entrance. Doyle then commented on the strange decision of Costa Coffee to renovate their premises during the Canton Fair. She thought both of these issues were of little concern and that he spent too much time talking about things that were inconsequential. She again admonished Doyle about eating too quickly and about his table manners.

They left and stood outside for a while talking. She then declared she would have to stop scolding him and that she shouldn't be so judgemental. Soon after Sharon and he parted ways and went home. Doyle wasn't sure what to make of all Sharon's recent observations.

Sharon went to her hometown and Doyle went on holiday so they didn't meet for over a month. When he returned they had a discussion by text one evening around the idea that she didn't want to be his girlfriend. He was insisting he had never asked. He saw her a couple of days later. She arrived at his house late in the evening and had brought beer with her. He gave her a candle holder but she wasn't greatly impressed. She took a fancy for a Schu bag that she saw lying around and he said she could have that plus a little pendant he had bought at some foreign airport. She had two buns with her that she had baked but they were very pasty. Doyle put his in the electric dishwasher to brown it up but she ate hers as was. It was midnight when she left.

After that it was almost three months before Doyle saw Sharon again. They met at their old rendezvous, the Friendship Store, and she was late as usual but only by about five minutes. Of course she wanted to go walking. They walked under the railway bridge and up the hill and past the big BBQ until they eventually reached Luhu Lake.

It was earlier than usual for them and there were hundreds of people engaged in various activities on the big plaza in front of the art museum. Groups of people were playing cards, mahjong, ping pong, badminton and the game where they keep the shuttlecock in the air using only their feet. There were singers attended by crowds and children driving around on mechanized pandas, bears and lions. Many people were just sitting around watching.

Sharon said she was too tired to walk around the lake. So they turned and headed towards Xiaobei. When they got near there she bought a pineapple from a roadside stall. Then she got a phone call and Doyle had to carry the pineapple.

She said she wanted to go to a restaurant near Doyle's apartment. On the way, she spotted a new place which was just after opening and decided they would go there. It was a dumpling restaurant. First of all, they had some fungus which was so so. Then the dumplings came, and they were not delicious, to put it kindly.

Sharon declared these to be the worst dumplings she had ever tasted and that she would never set foot in the joint again. She blamed it on the two older ladies who were working there. This, despite the fact that there were two young lads there too. They left there and, as Doyle had already guessed, she wanted to go to McDonald's for ice cream. They didn't stay there too long before they headed on their respective ways. Again Doyle didn't hear from Sharon for some time until she texted one night to say she would be going away the next day to her hometown. He asked her if she was coming out to meet him, but she said it was too late. He was puzzled; lateness had never bothered her before.

Then she called Doyle. She got straight to the point. Her foreign friend had reappeared a while back and had begged her to meet. She agreed. Erik arrived and they had a very romantic evening. But when he left in a hurry the next morning as usual, she decided it was time to get to the bottom of this ongoing mystery.

She sounded calm and content, which puzzled Doyle. Usually, an encounter with her friend led to upset and anger. After this latest encounter she made a spur of the moment decision to ring him the following weekend. She had never called him at the weekend before, in fact she had hardly ever called him at all. He usually initiated contact.

Sharon was in for a shock. When she called a lady answered!!!!
"Can I speak to Erik?"
"I'm sorry. Erik is not in. Who can I say called?"
"My name is Sharon. I didn't know he had a partner!"
"I'm not his partner. I'm his sister. I live with him."
Sharon thought this strange. "Oh, sorry."
"I live with him because I'm disabled. I use a wheelchair. He promised our parents that he would always take care of me."
"Can you please ask him to call me? I apologise again."
Later that evening, Erik rang Sharon. There was no need for explanation, but he explained anyway and apologised for his strange behaviour over the previous period. Sharon now realised that they could never be together, but she understood. She wasn't

happy as such, but she felt at ease. Sharon went on to tell Doyle that she was going to her hometown and wouldn't be coming back. She wanted a clean break from her past and to make a new start.

"You see now, Joe. I always knew he was a good man!"

Doyle never saw nor heard from her again.

The Avon Lady

It doesn't matter whether you are young free and single or older, free and single again. If you are active in the game of romance, you are liable to meet all sorts of folk. Some are very nice, some not so nice, some off-the-wall, some dangerous and a few totally cuckoo. But perhaps one of the most remarkable encounters Tom Mitchell had was with a female he came to know as the Avon Lady.

"An Avon lady is an independent sales representative for a company called Avon. Using the company's catalogues, sales materials, and samples, an Avon lady sells makeup and skincare products as well as perfumes, colognes, and items intended for bathing and pampering. She may also sell the company's jewellery, clothing, toys, and novelties."

They had met online on some long-forgotten precursor of Tinder. As is usual in these situations, there were a few run of the mill messages exchanged. They provided each other with a minimalist kind of bio and later seamlessly moved on to discussing likes, dislikes, jobs, pastimes, hobbies, holidays and pets. After a decent amount of time had elapsed, a tryst was arranged.

Tom had retained some information about her, such as her name, age, size as well as the particulars of her teddy bear, Rufus. He had also come to know that this woman, Aileen, had a passion for dogs. She owned a number of purebred Collies and they competed at shows all over Ireland and occasionally beyond. Tom also learned that there was a cat among the canines. Meanwhile, Aileen had heard about his liking for sport, reading, walking, fly fishing and sudoku.

It was a few days before Christmas, and she appeared to be very much looking forward to this meeting. She had even talked about Tom coming back to visit her a second time before New Year. All before they had even met for the first time! This had given him some food for thought. After all, he had other plans and didn't want to be tied down to a big woman with a flock of dogs, a cat and a much-loved teddy bear.

Anyway, on the evening in question, Tom set off in hope but with mixed emotions and all sorts of thoughts tumbling through his head. She had told him she was 41 years of age and was clothes size 18-20. At that time, Tom knew little of ladies' sizes. He had tried to ask tactfully for more details about the size but with no great success in terms of a definitive answer.

Tom had talked to his teenage daughters about sizes earlier in the day. He began by asking them about their sizes in clothes and was told 10 to 12, but this led to complications. They thought he was going to buy them clothes and they were giving him great attention. He then took another tack and asked what size their mother was; they then thought he was going to buy clothes for her, but couldn't understand why, as they had been estranged for several years. She is usually a 12 he was told and sometimes a 10, depending. He didn't know what it depended on but was willing to believe what he was told. He was now getting a rough idea, though, of the girth of this potential match. From his perspective, it wasn't looking great, especially as he had a liking for slender ladies. The discussion then moved swiftly on to Aunt Peggy who Tom saw as a big woman.

"Oh, Aunt Peggy would be a 12 or 14, Daddy. Maybe a 16? Why do you want to know what size clothes Aunt Peggy takes,

Daddy?" Tom had to pretend he was just enquiring. Follow up questions continued for some time afterwards and it took a great deal of careful navigation to get off the subject without giving the game away.

It was already dark when Tom set off for the rendezvous. He had arranged to meet this lady of uncertain size at a designated roundabout in County Antrim, near the appropriately named Nutts Corner. The journey was uneventful, but Tom's imagination was on overdrive. His thoughts veered from extremely negative and apprehensive to a few expectant notions thrown in for balance. There were sweet, exotic, romantic reveries frequently interrupted by a jolt back to reality and the impending encounter with this probably plump partner. Of course she would be lovely and just slightly overweight, he reassured himself... but at other points he struggled to believe himself.

Tom arrived on time and sure enough there she was, sitting waiting in her grey estate car. He guessed this vehicle was an ideal dog transporter. He didn't dally. He got out and walked over to her car. As soon as he approached, she opened the window and he was met by the fumes and fragrance of Fido. She herself sat there silently taking stock of him. Tom looked in at her and, while the overpowering odour dominated his thoughts, he did notice that she was the full of the front seat, as wide as a gate and as big as a house. He casually asked if she had been waiting long but she dismissed his question replying that she had only recently arrived.

She asked if her potential partner would like to get in and so he walked round to the passenger side and gingerly sat in beside her. Tom's eyes unconsciously searched for dogs but though he could smell woman's best friend, he could see no physical presence. Aileen seemed to be on edge. She began ranting about a man who had parked beside her, then behind her and finally across from her in the course of the last few minutes and who she thought was acting a bit strange. When Tom arrived this person had apparently driven off. He had seen nothing and wondered if she had imagined it.

After she settled herself, they talked a bit, but he sensed there wasn't the slightest flicker of a spark, even at this early stage of acquaintance. Tom found nothing to latch on to at all and no doubt the feeling was mutual. But they were very polite and they talked of her ex, his ex and any other ex **they** could think of.

Even though he was totally uninterested, Tom asked her if she thought she was up for it - maybe she would send him away for being rude. But she didn't, although she did concede that she had doubts. Despite this small setback, she did suggest he follow her back to her place. So off they went and in 15 minutes or so, after a journey across the Antrim Hills, they arrived at her house in a town which was unfamiliar and unknown to Tom.

On arrival, she opened the door and went on in. Her reluctant date followed. The malodour of mutt was all-pervasive. While all was quiet for a few seconds, it wasn't long before Tom came face to face with this pride of pooches who had been kept outside while their mistress was away. As soon as she opened the back door in they thronged, swamping her, Tom and the cat, which ran for its life upstairs. He was jumped on and licked all over as the Avon Lady tried to restore calm. She then requested him to take a seat on the sofa in the lounge… alone with the dogs, while she made coffee. He obeyed but more in hope than confidence.

Inevitably, Tom came under a sustained attack again as he sat on the couch. Rufus endured a similar fate and looked like he would be decapitated before the evening was over. As Tom tried to fend off dogs large and small, he was trying to take in his surroundings. It was clearly a very doggy house. The walls were covered in a flowery wallpaper with a faded beige carpet on what could be seen of the floor. All the furniture was covered in sheets and he guessed this was to keep the dogs from tearing at the upholstery. There were dog bowls and old bones everywhere, various doggy and catty toys, scratching posts, balls and bundles of rags. There were doggie pictures on the walls with pennants and prizes from various dog shows all on display. Amidst all of this sat an ancient dusty TV on a battered brown coffee table.

The coffee came and then Tom got the full story on the different dogs; the complete CV for each of them. She began with the youngest dog, a four-year-old, who had recently been neutered. Unfortunately it hadn't had the desired effect of calming him down and he continued to run harum-scarum about the house. Tom was told how he wasn't suitable for shows and the reasons why; this, despite the huge amount of training he had undergone.

Then the 10-year-old bitch was introduced and Tom was shown her favourite toys, favourite hiding places and heard about some of her exploits with Farmer Jones's cattle, near the last house my friend had lived in. That was back in the days when Aileen had lived in a more rural area. A few years ago this girl had come second in the Green Star Bitch of the Year competition. Aileen then left temporarily but soon came back with two bowls of chilli con carne.

After a few more doggie bios, Aileen ended with the old dog, who was apparently deaf and could only see with one eye. He was 13 and well past his sell-by date. Tom thought he didn't have the configuration of a collie and, when he raised this issue, she confirmed his suspicions that this animal was indeed a mongrel. He had the head of a Labrador and was a reddish-brown colour. The other dogs were typical collies, black and white. Tom wondered how this mixed-race renegade would have been received at the dog shows his friend attended.

He was given a rundown of all this dog's achievements, his strengths and his vices. He was also informed that this senior citizen had recently become incontinent and that this was probably "a wee virus". It occurred to Tom that it was a good job it wasn't a big one. He asked why she didn't put the dog outside and soon realised that he had cooked his goose regarding any possible residual chance with Aileen. She flared again, just as she had when he first met her and he instinctively recoiled. It was too cold outside for the poor creature, she claimed angrily, he was too old. Oh, and he didn't cause much bother; she always put an old towel down at night for him to lie on and sure couldn't it go in the washing machine in the morning.

Then Tom was regaled with tales of the cat, although it's history had been less glorious than that of the dogs. There were only so many mouse hunting stories one could relate. Of course, there was the time puss had climbed a tree and wouldn't or couldn't return to earth. A neighbour had to go up a ladder that time and nearly fell out of the tree when he overreached himself. The said Felix hadn't been spotted since he had hurriedly disappeared upstairs when they had first arrived.

Aileen then moved on to talk about herself and her voice picked up as she described in detail all her ailments, including the abscess on her behind and the intestinal disorder she was afflicted with. Tom was getting less keen by the minute, if that was possible, and wondering more and more now how he could make an honourable exit at an appropriate time. He was still being probed and nuzzled by dogs on an ongoing basis but couldn't really go until after the chilli had been consumed.

His host had been sitting at the opposite end of the room all the while, so he had an inkling she was putting distance between them deliberately. He was a bit relieved really as the thoughts of the carbuncle and the bowel disorders were large in his mind. Even at this early stage he knew they would be the source of many future nightmares. He was devouring the chilli and he was sure, through her canine eyes, she saw him straining at the leash, such was his anxiety to flee.

It had also been emphasised once more that Aileen was an Avon lady and how she had made quite a bit of money out of that. Tom did mention that he had never actually come face to face with an Avon lady before. But, just as they got on to this topic, it reminded her that she had to deliver an order. It was a Christmas present and the customer had to have it. She didn't have time to bring it tomorrow, which would be too late in any case.

A shadow passed over her face as she considered this sudden emergency. Tom immediately saw this as his opportunity to extricate myself from this hound heaven. She was going to have to deliver this order very soon and he would then be able to safely make his escape. It may have been an exit strategy for her too. He would never know.

Again Tom asked her if she was up for it. Again it was involuntary. Perhaps he was unconsciously trying to move things on quickly to their inevitable conclusion. What would he have done if she had said YES? He was demanding rejection. Luckily she said NO. Tom pretended to be distraught but dignified in defeat whilst simultaneously struggling to keep his true feelings under wraps. Tom was under no pressure now, nor was she, so they started to talk about the online dating game again and the various people they had met. She told him she had met very few people but he wasn't sure if she was telling the truth. She did mention an encounter with one old boy who was ten years older than his given age and who used a walking stick. Tom mentioned a few people he had met including the semi-bald woman with a wig; tensions evaporated and they became great pals all of a sudden, promising each other to keep in touch.

As Tom was leaving he asked for directions back to where he had found her. She offered him two routes and then led him out into the night. As he passed the bottom of the stairs he looked up to see a rather doleful cat staring down from the landing into the doggy world below. On the doorstep he gave Aileen a fleeting peck on the cheek. They again promised faithfully to stay in touch!!

Not daring to look back, Tom slunk away to his car, dived in and drove off in a very relieved frame of mind. He was accompanied by the odour of dog for several miles until he had the presence of mind to squeeze the air freshener.

Saigon Slicker

Joe Doyle had been in Guangzhou for about eighteen months when Dutch Darcy came to visit. Dutch was on an Asian tour. Doyle met Dutch at the airport and after the lengthy immigration process was completed they travelled back to the city centre on the metro.

Dutch was in an upbeat mood. He was looking forward to their upcoming trip to Ho Chi Minh City (HCMC). The freedom of escaping from his partner had made him giddy. He was a different man now, Dutch the lady killer. In Ireland, he was the devoted family man. There it was all lovey-dovey stuff. "Yes, dear! What can I get you now dear?" holding hands, pecks on the cheek, and frequent hugs.

Dutch dumped his luggage, showered and wanted to go on the town. Doyle had arranged to meet a few friends at a favourite restaurant. Dutch loved the company and the multiplicity of courses. Later they progressed to a nearby bar where a good time was had by all. Dutch had lost his adrenalin rush and was now tiring. Everyone dispersed about eleven o'clock.

Next morning, after a late breakfast, Doyle picked Dutch up and they headed for Zhujiang New Town where they looked around the museum, the opera house and the library. Dutch was really knocked out by the design of the library and also by the whole concept of Zhujiang New Town.

In the late afternoon the two boys set off for the airport. Everything went smoothly and they arrived into Ho Chi Minh City (HCMC) about 1.30 am. Dutch had to wait for a visa, which took 30 minutes. Meanwhile, Doyle got some money changed.

Before they left the Arrivals Hall they were approached by a man they took to be a taxi driver who offered to bring them to their hotel. They asked no questions and were soon on their way. Too late they found they had been conned when they were charged about 40 USD - it should have been about 10 USD. Then he asked for a tip!!!

The next morning, a Saturday, they were up about 8.30 am. Breakfast was very good and there was great personal service from the very friendly staff. They met two Frenchmen who gave them a little advice about ladies, ladies in bars, over-friendly ladies etc. Dutch then asked these men about restaurants and they recommended two.

Later, the two lads went walking around the area. The first thing they sought out was the nearest Irish Bar which was only about 50 yards down the street (men do have to have some priorities). It was run by an affable Glaswegian whose parents hailed from Foxford in Co Mayo. He advised them on various things to do in HCM.

They resumed their walk and ended up at the river. Here they decided to go their separate ways for a while. Doyle went back towards the hotel and had lunch on the way. He read a bit but couldn't decide if he liked this book, *The Garlic Ballads*. It was heavy at times.

Dutch came back later and they talked for a while. After dark, they headed for dinner to a place which had been recommended by the Frenchman. It was really good. The ambience was good, there was music and the food was delicious. They progressed to the Irish Bar. The owner of the bar, Eddie, was a little distant with

Doyle this time because he was only drinking coffee. Dutch was knocking back the beer and Doyle left early. Dutch didn't return for a long time. Just as Doyle was thinking of going out to look for him he finally struggled in. Doyle was awake all night after having coffee so late in the evening. Things weren't helped by Dutch who snored and farted all night.

Doyle was up early and had breakfast alone. Dutch remained above. Afterwards, Doyle went out for a walk and had a massage. The girl was good at her job. Doyle was lying there getting his legs done, hot stones on his back and the rain rattling off the roof. It felt very homely in some way but in what way he wasn't sure. He went back to the hotel and discovered Dutch was still in bed.

When Doyle mentioned the noise during the night, Dutch got very defensive and maintained Doyle had been snoring too. Doyle was reminded now that Dutch was not a man to take criticism of any sort. He was always right. Because things had gone smoothly for a couple of days, Doyle had forgotten about another side of Dutch. This was his first huff!

In the afternoon, they went off on a city tour which included a Buddhist temple, the war museum, the presidential palace and a market. It rained throughout but the tour guide, the aptly named Typhoon, did much to keep them in good cheer. They were back at 6 o'clock. Dutch wanted to go to a restaurant that someone had recommended. Doyle didn't agree as these recommendations were all expensive and there was no need to do expensive in a city where every restaurant was good. Dutch then went off out in another huff. Doyle went to the noodle shop around the corner and had dinner there.

Later when things had cooled down they met up again and went to a few bars including a karaoke joint where they chatted to the hostesses. The happy outgoing Dutch now came into play. He was in his element. In this bar, customers usually bought a drink for themselves on arrival and then had the option of buying a drink for a chosen lady. For 20 dollars you could go upstairs to sing karaoke with a lady. The boys didn't bother with the karaoke but stayed at the bar and at closing time headed back to the hotel again.

On Monday, Dutch went off in a taxi to explore the history museum and the zoo. Doyle went for a long walk and spent about two to three hours outdoors looking around markets etc. Doyle came back again but there was no sign of Dutch. He read some more of Mo Yan's *Garlic Ballads* and he was now finding it a very depressing read. It kept getting worse .... should he continue to read it or drop it?

There was still no sign of Dutch at 6.30 pm. Doyle found somewhere to eat and had dinner. Eventually, Dutch did come back all excited. He said he had had an amazing day. He had gone off walking and then took a motorbike taxi. The driver had brought him all over the city.

Dutch described a visit to a museum, which was officially closed. He somehow managed to get in and followed a group of German tourists who were getting a private tour. Then he went to the zoo. He had just reached the deer pen when he encountered a young lady who insisted on bringing him off for a massage.

Dutch and the girl both had a massage, but she expected Dutch to pay for her too; he only wanted to pay for his own. He then went off with his taxi man and met another girl somewhere in a market and made a date to meet her on Tuesday evening. He was getting really worked up about this and went into a long detailed description of the girl in question.

Later they went to the karaoke bar and had a few drinks. It was mostly frequented by Japanese clients who liked to sing. The girls would go upstairs with them and serve them drinks while they sang - that was as far as it went. There were no extra services here. Doyle and Dutch chatted to two of the ladies. Dutch was still high and very excited. He had a few beers and Doyle had water.

Doyle was getting teased by the manager about Nhi, the girl he was talking to. He was going to marry her and there were discussions on the size of the ring, how many diamonds etc. Eventually, one of the other girls, the girl in green, made a ring from a piece of plastic and Doyle had to put this on his 'intended's' finger.

There were no clients in for the karaoke so the bar closed about 11 pm and the boys were put out. Doyle arranged to meet his new "wife" and the girl in green on Wednesday at 12 noon. Dutch wanted his girl to go off with him but she wasn't having that. She made an excuse and told him to come back on Wednesday night.

They went on back to the hotel, but Dutch was talking constantly about his recent experiences in a very excited and aroused state. He described every little detail of what had passed between the latest girl and himself and all the touching, feeling and rubbing that went on. Doyle wasn't too interested but to humour Dutch he pretended to listen as they walked back to the hotel.

On arrival at the hotel, Dutch immediately got into conversation with the porter. After these consultations, Dutch informed Doyle he had a girl coming to visit him and that Doyle couldn't go to the bedroom. Obviously this had been arranged earlier without Doyles' knowledge.

Dutch said he wouldn't be long. It was 90 minutes later before he reappeared. Doyle wasn't best pleased but said nothing. He realised that agreeing to share a room with Dutch was a grievous mistake.

Again Dutch was really excited and keen to tell Doyle all about it. Doyle didn't want to hear *but was well aware that you have to listen to thunder.* He was now very late to bed and they were up early in the morning for a trip to the delta.

Dutch had them up at 6.45 and a lengthy period was spent at

the mirror before they went out. Doyle had forgotten that Dutch was a vanity project. Even for this daytime adventure he was at it. He saw himself as a youthful Adonis type character while Doyle saw him as more of an ageing Narcissus. He would take over the bathroom for up to two hours while he stretched, shimmied and vibrated in front of the looking glass. Sometimes he hummed to himself as he applied all the various body lotions. This was accompanied by a running commentary on his hopes and aspirations for the time ahead.

They were picked up at the hotel. On the bus journey the tour guide kept talking in a very boring kind of way. He never shut up. He hated China and the Chinese for some reason and blamed them for the Vietnamese war with USA.

It took about an hour on the bus and then they got on a boat which took them out on the river. They went to an island where there were stalls everywhere selling trinkets. They drank special tea with rejuvenating powers. This was followed by a ride in a horse and cart across the island, which was mostly mangrove swamp interspersed with colonial houses.

They went on a smaller boat along a narrow waterway through the swamp, which gave them a feel of how it must have been for the Yanks in the '60s and '70s. There was a very nice lunch at a restaurant in a clearing. Then a journey back by boat and on to the bus again.

Dutch was again very high and for the usual reason. He had taken a fancy to one of the girls on the boat who was Japanese. He made several remarks about her and what he would like to do with her. He kept on about her even after they got off the bus and when he had exhausted that topic he turned to his 'date' later with a young woman he had met the day before. *Bathroom out of bounds this evening* thought Doyle.

On their return Dutch wanted to go to sleep for the rest of the afternoon. Doyle left him there and went off for a walk. He had a good look around town, bought a couple of souvenirs and found his way back eventually before going upstairs for a rest himself. Dutch had gone out in the meantime.

Doyle was reading a bit and sleeping a bit. Dutch then barged in in an awful humour giving out about being ripped off and many other ills. He had taken a taxi recommended by the porter and the taxi had driven him around for 40 minutes when his destination was just a short distance away. He demanded to be brought back to the hotel and then refused to pay the fare.

The taxi driver followed him inside and the receptionist had had to negotiate a settlement. Doyle found it hard to understand, the full details such was the bad temper Dutch was in. Worst of all the date had had to be cancelled. Dutch wasn't able to get there on time and the girl had stopped answering texts.

Dutch was almost shouting at Doyle as he narrated this story and before he had told it all, he stormed off for coffee. Doyle sat a while before deciding to follow him downstairs to see if he was in the coffee shop down the street. Indeed he was. Doyle ordered tea and joined him.

Dutch was all over the place emotionally. He was still very cross about the porter and also making lots of resolutions. His money would be spent exclusively on good food in the future. He told Doyle about this gorgeous, beautiful food he had just had earlier. There would be no more women! Doyle had heard most of it before.

The next minute, Dutch had thrown the switch again. He was planning on going to discos, karaoke bars and the like. Doyle couldn't follow this line of thinking. Dutch was talking, talking, talking. Doyle said to him that he should try and cool down and to be careful. Dutch then took umbrage and told Doyle he could look after himself and would take Doyle's advice and put it along with all the other advice Doyle had given him. Doyle just got up and walked out without saying anything and went back to the hotel. Dutch came back later and went off upstairs without speaking. Doyle sat downstairs for a while before going up, but Dutch was already in bed and apparently sleeping. Doyle read for a while before he went to sleep.

Doyle was up early and had a nice breakfast all alone. Dutch came down later. He was speaking but not saying very much. Doyle decided it was better to play along and not ignore him, which might have exacerbated the situation. Doyle was to meet his friend Nhi from the karaoke bar at 12 midday. He doodled about the hotel in the morning while Dutch went off soon after breakfast. Doyle asked him what time he would be back and he said he didn't know. Doyle guessed he would be OK by evening.

Doyle went off to meet Nhi and her friend, the girl in green. Her friend had a scooter and when Doyle arrived at the meeting point they were already there sitting on the scooter waiting for him. Once the scooter had been parked the trio went into a cafe and had lunch. Then they walked down to the Saigon River.

There were many small fish swimming around right next to the river bank. Nhi caught a fish and took it out of the water in her hands She put it in a throwaway plastic food container and put some water in on top of it as it flopped around. After playing with it for a while she put it back in the water and it swam leisurely away.

It came on to rain very heavy and they had to take shelter in a nearby cafe. Doyle had tea, Nhi had coconut juice. Kim, the girl in green, had a cold latte plus a big heap of ice cream topped with fresh cream and served in an coconut shell. When the rain stopped they walked back to the scooter and the girls headed home to prepare for work.

Doyle went back to the hotel. He met Dutch who was on his way to have a massage upstairs in the hotel. Doyle said he would go outside for one himself. Just across the road down an alleyway he found a place and had a massage there. The girl was nice, she was good at her job and she chatted away all the time without being too much.

When Doyle came back, Dutch was getting ready for a scooter tour of the city. He asked Doyle if he would go too. Doyle said he would leave it. He explained that it would be too much for him. He didn't want to go to bars and he didn't want to get too high. Dutch went on ahead and was happy enough with the situation. Doyle went for a walk around an outdoor market.

Doyle found a nice souvenir shop on the way back and bought three lacquered candle holders in black, each with a golden dragonfly. These were for his daughter. He also bought a book, *The Master and Margarita*. He had earlier finished *The Garlic Ballads*. which had been a series of disasters. He was glad to be out of that book. It had seemed to coincide with Dutch's humour for a few days and the two were interlinking so much that reality and fantasy pretty much felt the same.

Dutch came back and wanted to go to the karaoke bar to chat with the lady friend with whom he had made a date on his last visit. But he had to ready himself which could take between one and two hours. "Mirror mirror on the wall." Doyle went on ahead and the girl who owned the bar gave him a glass of Vietnamese wine which tasted like poitin. The girls were wondering where Dutch was. He eventually came much later and smelt like a small pharmaceutical factory

The atmosphere was good. Doyle thought Dutch might do karaoke but he didn't and they stayed in the bar. The girl Dutch had arranged to meet didn't turn up although there were plenty of others to distract him. As the karaoke wound down most of the girls started drifting off home about 11 pm. Doyle soon followed but Dutch stayed behind to chat with the owner and another girl, and to drink Tiger.

The next morning Dutch set off on a tour of the Vietcong tunnels. After breakfast Doyle went back to bed and had a sleep. It was comforting to listen to the rain beating off the windows. Later he went out and had lunch. The heavy rain continued and he retreated back to the hotel. He casually wondered how Dutch was getting on in the tunnels. Were they flooded out?

Dutch came back and was planning to go to a restaurant he liked and also to a bar where there was music. He was meeting a lady who Doyle guessed was a hooker. Dutch really went overboard on dressing up for the occasion and there were all kinds of aftershaves and sprays applied to his torso, neck and face as he writhed and wriggled in front of the reflector. Doyle lay on the bed laughing.

"Dutch you could turn up in a pair of dirty boots, working clothes without having had a shower for weeks and you would still get the same reception from a hooker. All they are interested in is the money." Dutch didn't react to this dose of reality. He heard nothing such was his state of euphoria.

Doyle said he would take it easy and not go too far. He went up the street to a restaurant that he had seen during the day. It was very big and capable of taking 200-300 customers. He called this one The Principality Stadium as it had a retractable roof which could be pulled over when it rained and left open when it was dry, letting out all the vapours and smoke.

After eating, Doyle returned to the hotel. Dutch had still not gone out. He had just appeared downstairs, fresh from his ablutions and sporting a very flowery shirt. He said it was his last night in town and he wanted to make the most of it. He certainly looked ready for action and soon headed off.

Doyle went to the coffee shop next door and drank jasmine tea, ate apple crumble and read his book. Later he visited the karaoke bar. All the girls were there, but they were busy upstairs attending to customers. After a while, when the karaoke finished, they came down and sat at the bar with him until 11.30. He told them he was leaving the next day. When he was leaving they all came out to the door to wave him goodbye.

On Doyle's return there was no sign of Dutch so he went to bed and read. The book was gripping with many strange and interesting characters, including the Devil. Some time after Doyle had gone to sleep, Dutch rushed in and declared that he had a girl with him. This time Doyle was relieved to discover Dutch had booked another room. Off he went armed with condoms and a toothbrush. Doyle guessed it was about 1.00 am and went to sleep again.

Doyle was woken again by Dutch at 6.45 am. He was talking about the great night he just had. He was in a state of high excitement and mentioned heavenly bodies, an ass to die for and the best night of his life. He revealed that he had been joined by a third party during the night. Doyle couldn't help but wonder if one polished his shoes while the other ironed his shirt.

Dutch needed money now to pay for his extravaganza. He rummaged through the safe without finding anything. He then asked if Doyle had 100 dollars. Doyle said he only had 20. Dutch said he would have to go to the bank but it had all been worth it. He ran out again leaving the safe door lying open.

Doyle got up soon afterwards, closed the safe door, and went for breakfast followed by a walk. It was a lovely morning. Dutch was hardly likely to surface for some time and would definitely miss the breakfast. He had talked about getting all the badness out of his system and even admitted that there was no fool like an old fool during his early morning visit to the safe. Doyle wondered what his sentiments would be later when he had rested ... a retraction of all his virtuous intentions, Doyle surmised.

In the afternoon, they got ready for the airport. They gave tips to the staff and headed off in a taxi. They were only charged 10 dollars this time. They were a little behind schedule so it was goodbye to the duty-free and straight on board. After they got airborne Doyle read all the way. Dutch blindfolded himself and put on his blowup collar.

It was dark when they landed and they went straight through immigration and customs without a hitch. They were on the metro in no time and went directly to Dutch's hotel.

Doyle soon saw that Dutch hadn't quite got all the badness out of his system as preparations for another night out were soon under way. The "old fool" headed straight to the bathroom to admire himself for a prolonged period whilst he shaved, showered and sprayed. Doyle prepared himself to be dazzled by the flowery shirt and maybe even the dancing shoes.

The Flight from Bucharest

I was on my way back to Ireland from Bucharest after spending ten days there. I was relaxed and well prepared for the journey. I could look back on memories of Romania, had a book to read and had a few hours in Milan Malpensa to look forward to.

I found myself seated beside a middle-aged Englishman who soon engaged me in conversation and introduced himself as Alan. He said he was from Uttoxeter. I told him I had heard of this place; it had a famous racecourse. I knew it was somewhere between Stoke and Derby. He agreed about the racecourse, but he had no interest in horse racing.

Alan was returning from Romania and it turned out he was an intrepid traveller. He seemed keen to talk and sounded interesting. In his time, he had been all over Romania, Bulgaria, other parts of Eastern Europe and Turkey. He also informed me he had driven Route 66 in the United States, made famous by one Bob Dylan.

He assured me that he had a lot of friends in Romania and was returning after spending some time with them. These included his girlfriend, who lived with her mother and an orphaned gypsy girl. He went on to talk about his girlfriend and how he had first met her in Turkey a couple of years before. He didn't describe the circumstances of meeting her, but he had come to the rescue of this dishevelled and beaten up young woman who was fleeing from a violent Turkish husband. Alan was keen to describe the whole episode around her escape. They had been arrested at the airport as he attempted to help her flee from the Turkish man. In the end they somehow did manage to wheedle their way out of it. Again he was light on detail, but I guessed this came after a handsome sum of money had changed hands. Following their safe arrival in Romania, he ended up staying for a month in Bucharest with the girl, the mother and the orphan.

He went on to confide that he liked younger women. Alan had no time for ladies of his own age and said he wouldn't feel comfortable with an older model on his arm. He had been married back in the day but was divorced for several years. He then admitted that he wouldn't find a younger woman easily in his own country. He did say that he wished he were my age again.

That morning there was already a surreal feeling in the air and so I had no problem taking this yarn in my stride. I had just finished reading *The Life of Pi,* a novel of faith, friendship and perseverance.

My new friend went on to reveal that since the first encounter, he had been a very regular visitor to Romania. The girlfriend lived in Bucharest, but her family came from close to the Danube near Constanta. This is where they usually went when he visited and he described the house, or rather houses, these people lived in.

The family had two houses, one of which was used for sleeping in, while the other was used for daytime activities like cooking and working. They always ate outside unless it was raining. He described the life there as being idyllic in many ways, but he did say that he was often bitten in bed at night by what he thought were ticks or lice.

When Alan came on a visit the family often went off for trips in their donkey cart. They and their neighbours piled in with lots of food, fishing gear and beer (which he would buy) and they would head down to the banks of the Danube. He remarked that the donkey was very badly treated. The poor ass just didn't seem to be able to go fast enough and the Romanians would whip him constantly.

They would journey for about twelve km across rugged terrain and then through a forest until they came to their favourite spot by the river. On arrival, a net would be brought out and fishing would commence. A BBQ would be lit and while the food was cooking they would start on the beer. The feasting would go on all day and according to him the craic was mighty!

Alan then went on to describe the journey back in the evening. There would be great merriment and they would sing all the way. He described how their party was crossing a field on one occasion when suddenly they pulled up and the men got off and piled a load of weeds into the cart. He asked his girl if they were for the animals but was assured they were not... It was marijuana.

When they got back the weed was taken off, tidied up into bundles and put up into the rafters of the house to dry. At that point it suddenly dawned on Alan that this was what the local men were smoking constantly. Previously he had paid no heed. In fact he thought it was tobacco roll-ups they were puffing on.

The family kept cattle, pigs and chickens. One day before he left they had killed a pig. The axe used to execute the pig was the same one they used to chop wood. The next day, soup was on the menu and he found a piece of the pig's jawbone floating in it.

This led us on to a wide-ranging discussion on the food in Romania and the poor standards of hygiene. According to Alan, the food in the shops was poor, food in the restaurants was poor and the food in hotels wasn't good either. He told me that chickens' heads and feet were part of the staple diet and were sold in most shops. I thought it sounded like Asia. Indeed these items were probably eaten as normal outside the western bubble.

My new acquaintance ruminated on the nature of the Romanian people. From his observations, they seemed not to be motivated at all and there was little attention to the maintenance of property or vehicles. We surmised that it could have been lack of funds or the fondness of weed. The conversation ended abruptly as we landed in Milan. We disembarked and went our separate ways.

In Milan, the first thing that struck me was the number of black people wandering about. Usually I would pass no remarks on this fact, but it struck me now because I had seen no black people while in Romania. Then there were the herds of Koreans wandering around. They were small, excited people, they all seemed to be wearing a lot of makeup and some of the most awful looking clothes combined with the oddest hairstyles imaginable. Very garish altogether!

Indians strolled around the airport as if this was what they did every Saturday morning. An old Englishman dressed in a safari suit ambled around looking as if he was making do as best he could in this strange place. A Chinese man sat studiously reading the *Financial Times*. Well-dressed Italian ladies paraded around looking very demure. Shades and high heels were obligatory.

In body, I was in Malpensa, but in spirit, I was far removed. I was on the banks of the Danube fishing with Alan, enjoying the BBQ, flogging the donkey, smoking the weed, crunching the pig's jawbone, being bitten by the ticks and helping a girl flee from the clutches of an abusive Turkish husband.

The Foreign Expert

In April 2012, I went to work in China. I had a two-year contract with GWE (Great Wall English). My contract was for 22 hours a week and so I had quite a lot of free time. So after a few months when I had settled in and was feeling comfortable in my job I started looking for extra work.

I went around a lot of small English schools and training organisations dropping in my CV. As a result of this I did get a few hours here and there in schools or tutoring people privately, both kids and adults.

One day I got a call from a guy named Jerry who had seen my CV. He invited me to his office, interviewed me and said he would come back to me when an opportunity arose. He was Chinese, had apparently spent time in the USA and his English was very good.

I didn't hear from Jerry again for a week or two, but then one afternoon he called and asked if I was available to go to Panyu the following morning for four hours. He went on to explain the nature of the job.

The first thing he told me was that it wasn't a teaching job. I was to go to a company and be present while the company received prospective customers. I would pose as an English speaking foreign expert. In theory the clients would be greatly impressed to see that the company had foreign expertise.

Jerry asked me if I would be comfortable in this role. I assured him that it would be no problem. He reassured me that I didn't have to actually do anything apart from being present. There would be another westerner there fulfilling the same role. I would be picked up at the Garden Hotel at 7.40 am, taken to the factory and driven back afterwards.

He went into some detail. When we arrived at the company, I would be installed in an office as a foreign expert. Again he stressed I wouldn't have to do anything, just be present there along with the other westerner. The company would have groups of buyers coming and they wanted to impress these clients by showing that they had foreign experts on hand.

My job would be to sit there behind a desk, greet and shake hands with whoever was brought into "my office." The clients would not be English speakers, so there was no need for small talk or indeed to speak at all.

I was to be collected by Hugo, a driver for this company. I looked forward to it all in one way as it was impossible to guess what might happen. I had a suspicion that my biggest difficulty could be dealing with the food; lots of hens' feet, maybe even dog meat!! I prepared my best suit and determined to be on my best behaviour.

I was up at 7.00 am, shaved, dressed and ate a few dumplings for breakfast. I then set off for the Garden Hotel to meet Hugo and Eric by 7.40 am. Jerry had left instructions to meet them at the front door, but when I arrived, I realised there was no front door as the entrance was closed for renovation. However, I went around to the side gate and they were there.

Eric was a tall bespectacled American with a small goatee beard wearing wrist beads and carrying a bus conductor's bag. Hugo was a bald, red-faced, portly, thirty-something Chinese guy. The two boys spotted me coming and turned to greet me. We had barely introduced ourselves when our car pulled up and we all boarded.

En route we discovered that Hugo, the driver, was the sales director of the company we were going to.

I got talking to Eric in the car and I learned that he had been in Guangzhou for three years. I asked him which company he worked for, but he indicated that he had no regular job at present. He had been working part-time in various places but was now looking for a permanent post. He had been doing some small teaching jobs for Jerry and informed me that Jerry was in fact an ABC (American born Chinese) from Texas.

Eric then told me he had been all over South East Asia and had spent quite a bit of time in Indonesia, including East Timor. He said, though, that the place was full of UN workers. There was big money there for teaching English, but the cost of living was expensive because the presence of so many UN people had driven prices up. He informed me that the people there ate with their hands. The highlight of his visit was when he was offered dog's head soup. He didn't say whether he accepted!

According to Eric, he had driven around Indonesia on a motorcycle and had only come off once. He described that event as he had hit a patch of oil, skidded and dropped the bike, with him and the girlfriend on board. The worst part was not the fact that he had been slightly injured or that his Indonesian girlfriend had taken a knock but that a crowd of onlookers had sat there laughing and didn't offer any help whatsoever.

He didn't like Jakarta. He said that you weren't even safe walking along the sidewalks. If there was heavy traffic, motorcycles would just mount the pavement and drive along it. He also described the services in the suburbs as being very poor with open sewers, poorly paved roads etc.

Eric maintained that the motorcycle was handy as there was no need for tax or insurance, but you did have to wear a helmet. He regretted that he couldn't have a motorcycle in China because of the regulations in Tier 1 cities where motorcycles were banned.

This conversation had been sparked by the fact that as we approached Panyu, there were a lot of motorcycles on the road. While they are banned in most of Guangzhou, they are allowed down there. Eric explained that Panyu was a very old city, although now it was just a suburb of Guangzhou (containing 2-3 million people). Traditionally there had been a lot of artists in the city, dating back hundreds of years.

We got stuck in a traffic jam somewhere approaching Panyu and the driver then left the main road. We travelled along back streets and through green areas where farmers were tending to various crops. We crossed and recrossed the Pearl River.

Eventually, we arrived at our destination and were shown inside the reception area. Hugo, the driver, then took us around the boardroom and the showrooms where the company's products were displayed. They were in the suspended metal ceilings business and their name was Grampian Group Gmbh.

This company also had offices in Hong Kong, Singapore and Germany. After being shown around the offices, we were taken on a tour of the factory. It was a very clean and well-organised workplace – no sweatshop here. The workers all wore orange overalls and for some reason I thought of Guantanamo Bay. But the atmosphere was good and the 200 or so workers seemed to be going about their work very happily.

After this tour of the works we went back inside to the office and were taken upstairs. We were introduced to Johnson, the CEO, Kevin from Sales and Marketing, and an older guy Stephen who had come up from Hong Kong. We drank tea with these men before being shown to our respective offices.

I was to be vice president in charge of exports and Erik was to be head of research and development. My office was big with a huge desk, a comfortable swivel chair for me, several other chairs and a nice sofa against the back wall. There were numerous paintings on the walls and two huge filing cabinets behind me with glass doors, more like dressers than anything. There was an air conditioning system in place, hot and cold drinking water and automatic blinds on the windows which slid up and down depending on the angle of the sun at any particular time.

Erik and myself were allowed time to settle into our respective offices. I was to be a Dutchman, Frank Riijkind, VP of the company and in charge of exports and overseas sales. I was given a name badge which went around my neck, and a box of my business cards was put on the desk.

I was given detailed instructions by Johnson as another couple of executives stood by. The first group of visitors were to be from a company which was fitting out a new subway station in Beijing. When they arrived, my job would be to shake hands with everyone and say hello.

After I had been inducted everyone left except Stephen. He explained that he was a consultant for the company. He and I chatted for some time and I figured he wanted to find out about me. He was a well-read man with a wide knowledge of many things, not least suspended metal ceilings and partitions. He told me he was the expert on these in China and had worked all over Asia as well as with a company in Chicago a few years ago. He gave me his card and I gave him mine. While we chatted, I was trying to get into my computer, but it was difficult to get it going and eventually, I gave up.

Stephen told me that Chinese customers never came on time and said this was one of the reasons he preferred Hong Kong. He said that they had learned good habits from the British.

My new colleague then informed me that he had only been summoned to this meeting last night and had to postpone a meeting in another city until this afternoon and faced another four-hour drive to get there. He had left home very early, driven to the border, parked his car, walked across the border, got picked up by a driver and taken here; a journey of four hours altogether.

He spoke a lot about the Americans and how Apple and Microsoft had patented everything and were cleaning up on that. He told me that a factory making Apple phones only got 20% of the money. His point was that Chinese people were inventing many things but getting no patent rights or rewards.

He and I chatted away until finally, word came that the customers were coming. We had plans of the subway station out on the desk and were perusing them and chatting when the posse arrived. Actually there were only two guys accompanied by three of our management team, including Johnson. Everyone shook hands and greeted each other and then they went off again to their next port of call. That was it!

The second set of buyers didn't even bother coming to visit us. We had to sit on though until all these people had left as it wouldn't look good to see the whole panel of experts up and leaving by car halfway through the morning.

Eventually, the visitors did go and we were to go to lunch before being dropped back to Guangzhou. Hugo was joking about whether we would enjoy eating the dog meat and what kind of dog we would prefer. This was because people in Guangzhou believed the residents of Panyu were very partial to a bit of dog.

We set off in the car, and the mood was good. Soon we arrived at the restaurant, and the driver said that we would sit at a table outside. The restaurant was situated in the shadow of a huge bridge spanning the Pearl River. We were taken to a terrace along the river and seated in a covered area, open to the sides. There was a great view out over the river. It was a hot day and there were fans going everywhere, so it was tolerable. The man said we would be having seafood.

As soon as we were seated, the tea and Coke started flowing. Huge barges passed up and down constantly, some loaded to the gunwales and others going back empty. I imagined this was akin to sitting on the banks of the Rhine, although I had never had that experience personally.

We saw a big passenger cruiser coming downriver, but it pulled into a jetty before it reached us. There were barges loaded with containers and all kinds of unknown goods. Mixed in with all these were sand boats and fishing boats. There were many barges pulled up on the land across from us, and I assumed it was a dockyard of some sort. A helicopter flew low across the river.

The food came. There had already been a couple of appetisers, small bowls of cucumber and peppers with dressing. We started off with a big bowl of soup. The waitress ladled it out into smaller bowls. I didn't recognize the taste, but there was meat inside of an undetermined animal. It was good, so I supped away.

Then came shrimps, but they had to be peeled, which was a nuisance. The Chinese suck them and spit out the casings. I tried to shell them first, but it was a mess, and Erik said it was easier to do it the Chinese way.

Following the shrimps, we had fried fish, and that was followed by pineapple buns and a plate of mussels in sauce served inside big shells. These were always delicious. I ordered a bowl of rice and drank plenty of tea and Coke. I thought I heard Hugo tell Erik that we would only be paid for two hours. Erik seemed to take it in his stride and just said we would talk to Jerry when we got back. I said nothing.

We came away from there with bellies well filled. We seemed to go back the same way we came, although it was a different driver this time. This guy drove a lot slower. Another helicopter flew over as we drove along.

We passed the farms, the factories, the duck ponds and the fish farms and crossed the river a few times again. Erik and myself discussed the food we had had, and we wondered if there had been dog in that soup.

It took quite a while to get back to Guangzhou. The driver dropped us near the Zoo, and we walked back along the road a bit to Jerry's office, which was upstairs in a building there. I went to the toilet on the way in while Erik went on ahead.

Jerry was a tall guy for a Chinese, and when I entered, he was in there speaking with Erik and a student. They were busy discussing the girls' education. After a while, he got round to talking to us re the day's work. Erik started on about being away for six hours etc. After hearing this, I told him I had an agreement to be paid for four hours, and that was what I wanted.

There followed a long rambling story about Hugo mistakenly agreeing to pay us for two hours. I didn't buy it. Then he suddenly agreed to bring us to the bank. He actually paid me for four hours at 170 RMB per hour after agreeing on 150 earlier. I wasn't going to object. It was about £85.

When Jerry went back to his office, I spoke to Erik about this episode. He said it was always like this and best to just negotiate. He thought I had been a bit direct. I said I was in a hurry and hadn't time for bargaining. We took the subway back to Taojin.

I went on home to get ready for my proper work, and still wondering about the contents of the soup.

The Master

Big Joe Doyle was walking aimlessly down the street in Xianyang, not entirely sure where to go or what to do. His instinct was to keep walking, but his foot was hurting him. He had it in his head to either go to King Coffee and drink tea,, or else he could go for a foot massage to ease the pain.

As he walked on, the discomfort grew. He came to the foot massage clinic first, and that decided it. He had had foot massages before but had never visited this establishment. However, he had passed it many times and knew it to be well attended. On this occasion, it looked especially warm and inviting, and it didn't look to be too busy.

The clinic was set back off the road by about 20 metres with a big paved area to the front. Doyle entered through the sliding door and, on entering, saw that there was a small group of people inside.

The first person who came to his attention was a dapper little man in a white coat, which was several sizes too big for him. He couldn't make up his mind whether this fellow resembled Mr Bean or Kenneth Williams.

This man was treating a lady who was lying on her back on a bed. Another lady was lying on the bed next to her and all three were busy chatting. There were only four beds altogether. Two of the beds seemed to have a contraption which could raise them up at one end.

Work was suspended while Doyle was welcomed in. Everyone was speaking Chinese to him, and he understood little. After the initial greetings, Doyle was referred to a female therapist, a neat little lady with a big smile. She gestured to him to lie down on the bed next to the door.

There was a fish tank beside him containing a great number of brightly coloured small fish. High up on the wall opposite the beds was a large TV screen which was turned off at the time. After he was settled, the lady went off to prepare what was necessary for his massage.

Below the TV was the drinking water dispenser and beyond that a cupboard which contained various items like towels, oils and other paraphernalia for the job in hand. The walls were covered in white wallpaper with a light blue stripe. On the wall near the door was a prominently placed notice giving details of treatments and prices. Doyle had a quick look and figured his treatment would be 58 RMB ie about £6.

When his therapist returned, she beckoned him to sit down on a stool at the foot of his bed. A tub of hot water was brought in and his feet inserted. From previous experience, he recalled various flavours being added to the water, often rose petals. Here it was just plain hot water.

While his feet were soaking, the therapist buzzed about and drifted in and out of the conversation between the other three. After ten minutes or so, his feet were removed from the water and put up on a stool while the therapist dried them off with a towel. He was then instructed to lie on the bed while she got to work. Like the other patients, Doyle was free to chat, read or play with his phone while the massage was in progress.

She began with his knees and worked on down to his shins. Her fingers went into places previously untouched by human hands. Then she started on his feet. She looked so small and puny but in reality, was very strong and started digging her fingers deep into his feet. It wasn't too uncomfortable, and he was texting and relaxing as she worked.

After a while, an important-looking older lady with a mannish face came in. Doyle could see that she was inspecting the premises whilst taking off her coat. She was humming to herself as she busied herself about the place leading him to think she was the owner. Someone passed a remark about him. He could hear Ireland being mentioned.

The patient next to him was finished and put on her coat. Then the important lady went to the fish tank. She caught one fish and put it into a paper cup but failed to catch any more. The man in the white coat then came to her aid. He caught another couple of fish and added them to the cup, which had enough water to sustain the fish for a short while. The cup was then placed into a plastic bag which was knotted and presented to the departing customer.

As that customer left, another woman in a green and white dress arrived. The man in the white coat turned his attention to her but was keeping an eye on Doyle's masseuse all the time. Everybody knew each other, and there was great chat and joviality between all comers. Then the woman who looked like the owner handed Doyle her phone. There was an English speaking lady on the other end.

This caller demanded to know who he was, where he was from and why he was here. After receiving all this information, she told him that the purpose of this clinic was to improve health and wellbeing and that she was a customer herself. Doyle told her he had a foot problem which he hoped they might be able to deal with.

The lady explained that the man in the white coat was the owner, known far and wide as 'The Master' and an acknowledged expert in this field. The important-looking woman who Doyle thought was the owner was The Master's wife. His therapist was called Snow.

Doyle handed back the phone and instructions were relayed through The Master's wife to Snow. The Master went outside to smoke a cigarette. Doyle could see him through the glass door as he strolled around in front of the building chatting with the neighbouring shopkeepers, their customers, passers-by and the mahjong players at a nearby table.

At times the massage hurt a little, but generally, it was soothing and relaxing. A lady of about 40 then entered, came up to him and addressed him in English. It was the woman he had spoken to on the phone. She introduced herself as Anna and translated a few things between himself, Snow and The Master. She reiterated that he was a master of this practice, and Snow was training under him to learn the skills of the local massage.

The massage lasted about an hour, and the time passed quickly. Doyle was given a signal that he was all done and then paid the bill. As he was putting on his shoes, they asked if they could take photos with him. There was great excitement as he had selfies taken with everyone, in different combinations. He exchanged phone numbers with some of them.

Before leaving, Doyle visited the toilet and could see that the premises had two big rooms. The bathroom was along a corridor on the left and had a sink, toilet and a big water heater. At the end of the corridor was the second room where some more beds were visible. As he left the Master's wife escorted him to the door.

That evening, Doyle received pictures from two of the ladies as well as some promotional material telling him how good foot massage was for the circulation of the blood and indeed for all bodily functions. There was also mention of a membership card. He promised he would come back soon.

After that, Doyle went off on holiday to Chongqing, and so it was a couple of weeks before he returned for further treatment. When he arrived, there was no customer there, just The Master himself, his wife and Snow. The wife was lounging on a bed and The Master was sitting on a low stool. They changed the TV over to CCTV5 English language news. Just for him!

The procedure began and they texted each other a bit using their online translators to communicate. While The Master began working on Doyle, the wife was lolling on the bed, texting and laughing to herself. After a while, she went into the back room where she started to sing. Doyle later discovered that singing was her great passion.

On this occasion, The Master was quite gentle to begin with. Overall it wasn't too painful apart from a few stingers. Snow was there cleaning the fish tank, removing some material and changing the water. The water drawn off was used to water the plants around the front door. The Master was slightly distracted from the business at hand as he directed the cleaning.

As Doyle was about to leave, who should arrive but his very good friend and colleague, Ms Fan? That was a surprise. He didn't know she was a patient there. She sat down beside him and translated some points that the Master wanted to communicate to him.

Fan told him that she had only recently started treatment herself. The Master had identified her problems and also Doyle's. Hers were severe and she had booked 50 sessions for 2000 RMB (£250). His problems were not so bad. She said that, as well as the foot, The Master had identified some issues with his lower back and his shoulders, which he was indeed aware of.

The next day he was back. The Master was busy with a male customer, and so it fell to the wife to look after him. She was much more severe than The Master, and it was excruciating at times. The male customer left and a woman came. The Master was doing her feet, and before long, she was yelping, so Doyle guessed she must have had some serious problems. Fan then arrived. She knew the other lady and sat next to her on a bed two down from him. The woman was still in great pain while the master was working on her, and at times, she would jump up with her face twisted in agony.

At this point, Doyle was on a trial six-day course recommended by The Master, for which he got a block discount. He had The Master's wife for two days in a row and thought she was a bit rough. Fan confided that she wasn't considered quite as expert as The Master himself.

That was a tough period. Fan and Doyle went together a lot of the days. One day, The Master, too, was fairly rough with him. Fan was there, and she was laughing at his contortions and face pulling. In his most painful moments, Doyle was threatening to kill The Master.

Next thing, The Master left him and switched over to Fan. The wife started on Doyle, and she was worse than The Master. He was really suffering and making death threats to The Master's wife as well as The Master. Fan thought it was very funny, but it wasn't long until the Master had her leaping around and howling. It was a torrid afternoon, and it really did feel like the 'House of Pain'.

Despite all this, Doyle saw The Master as a comical-looking character lost inside his big white coat. Sometimes he would laugh when Doyle shouted out with pain. Such a sadist!!! Just as Doyle was sure he wanted to kill him, The Master would look at him as he sat there smiling with the look of a man who wouldn't hurt a fly.

The Master was a restless character. If there weren't many customers around, he would fidget a lot, sit awhile next to the fish tank, go outside to smoke or just walk around. He might lie down on a bed for a while and read one of the women's magazines which were always lying around. If Snow was treating Doyle he would be keeping one eye on her. The Master and his wife did give good tips on general health. On one occasion, Doyle's elbow was bothering him. The Master had a look at that and did some massage on the arm, which actually worked wonders. The wife was always advising against drinking any cold liquids. Chinese people seldom drink anything cold.

The massage varied every day, and The Master would often introduce something new, allied to the old reliables. The different pains and sensations became more familiar, and Doyle could never figure out why his left foot always hurt a lot more than the right. Sometimes the sensation would go up through his whole body, right to the crown of his head.

When the treatment was over, it was always a time of great relief. If The Master was in good humour, he would slap Doyle on the ankle, shout "OKAY" and hand him a paper cup filled with warm water. If there was another customer waiting Doyle had to pour the water himself.

Doyle discovered through time that The Master was in the business of selling goldfish and that a massage could be interrupted if he had to deal with a fishy customer. The fish had to be caught and put into a bag, cash taken and change given. Fan told him that they also owned a shop elsewhere where the bulk of the goldfish was traded.

The wife was probably the one with the main eye for business. She was a great woman for making money, and as well as the massage and goldfish businesses, she was also into selling ladies lingerie. The bras, pants etc were sometimes put on display on the seating opposite the massage beds.

The Mistress was as cute as a fox, too but likeable at the same time. After his initial trial period, Doyle bought a block of 10 treatments for about £40. When it came to the ninth day, she was all over him, with a great welcome on arrival and later giving him apples, peanuts and various other novelties to make sure he renewed.

The lady just loved to sing and often would lie on one of the beds recording herself. However, her voice wasn't the most melodious. Fan described her as having the voice of a jackdaw and the face of a horse. She was also a keen card player, and every afternoon without fail, she disappeared down the street for a few hours to play with a group of friends.

Summer came, and Doyle was leaving China. His last day at The Master's was an eventful one. He was again being attended to by Snow while The Master was with another lady on the first bed. Doyle was on bed 3 as usual, and The Master's wife was lying on bed 2 gossiping with the lady customer, texting Doyle and using the translator.

Just as Doyle's treatment was winding down, all of a sudden, there was a loud bang in the washroom. The Master ran down the corridor and opened the door to be met with clouds of steam and black smoke. The water heater had malfunctioned.

The place was busy, and a row of sedentary ladies began to cough and splutter. The Master tried to regulate the boiler but only succeeded in making it worse. The black smoke was billowing everywhere and soon filled the hall and then the treatment room. The only thing visible was the ghostly white figure of The Master flitting back and forward through the haze.

The Master's wife broke off in mid-verse, jumped off her bed and bolted for the door. Barefoot ladies fled the clinic and gathered outside on the street. Doyle, too, escaped in the pandemonium, shoes in hand.

Eventually, The Master got all doors and windows opened, and the boiler somehow righted itself. In the commotion, Doyle departed the scene unnoticed and without fanfare. His treatment was finished, and The Master had other fish to fry.

The smoke cleared a little to reveal The Master with his white coat now covered in black blotches. As he looked back all Doyle could see was a half-man, half-panda figure flitting through the smog!

The Road to "The Port"

"In all my dreams I seem to hear her sweet voice soft and low
I know she's waiting where we said goodbye in old Mayo."

The sun was shining and a blue sky stretched all the way to the horizon. The village was quiet, and I was still not fully in tune with this new day as I inhaled the crisp Saturday morning air. In about two hours time I should reach my destination. It was a familiar journey, but not one made recently nor one I was particularly looking forward to today.

A Garda car was parked halfway down the street, but the lawmen were nowhere to be seen. The village was slowly stirring to life. A battered, old green Toyota struggled up the hill, spitting and spluttering, jerking and jumping as it made its way onwards. It looked like a combination of age and a substantial injection of kangaroo petrol. Greg the gardener, still in recovery after a hard night singing in Tullys, was gingerly piloting the slow-moving vehicle. He had a trailer in tow, loaded with mowers, rotavators, rakes, forks, spades and hoes.

Two people in red parkas, who I took to be tourists, were loitering around the window of the estate agents. From the open door of Keogh's pub came the sounds and smells of breakfast cooking. I motored slowly on down the hill past the dormant internet café. A Boxer dog stood to attention outside Connollys.

He watched intently as Sexton's cat strolled down the far side of the street and hopped up onto a window sill. A family prepared to launch their cabin cruiser at the quay. All was well with the world.

Another busload of tourists had just discovered the castle. They were busy snapping the ancient edifice from all angles and distances, performing a wide variety of contortions in the process. Further along the road, I couldn't help but notice that there had been sweeping changes at what I knew as The Blue House. Previously, everything around the house used to match in a strange kind of way; there was the sky blue house itself, the powder blue wall along the road, the navy blue car in the drive, indigo flower pots at the front door, cyan curtains on the windows and a royal blue patio set. Now under new ownership, all blues had been banished, and the house painted a sickly green colour. It was hard to decide whether it was for better or worse.

At Ballyclera, an old fishing boat sat in the same roadside field where it has rested for years, like Noah's Ark, abandoned there high and dry. I wasn't sure whether it had once been painted a mauve colour or whether it was just covered in rust. Two retired bulldozers were parked nearby, with weeds and bushes growing up through them. They had stood there stoically for many years through upturns and downturns, like remnants of some extinct species doomed when they had failed to board the Ark.

Ballinderreen showed little sign of human activity. Just a few awkwardly parked cars outside a pub abandoned the night before and yet to be reclaimed. Two fat marmalade cats lay sunning themselves on the windowsill of a whitewashed cottage. As I waited at the T-junction by Mother Hubbards, a solitary Hell's Angel roared past on his ancient chopper. In Clarinbridge, another old boy in a pristine white Ford Anglia came sailing sedately over the bridge as if he was floating on air. A new Lidl supermarket had opened on the southern outskirts of Oranmore and was already a magnet for thrifty housewives. The string of horses of all shapes, sizes and colours, still grazed by the stream which flowed into the bay. Recently the herd had been infiltrated by a number of donkeys. At the other end of that village, the Quality Hotel once stood facing the Galway bound traffic. It still existed in body but no longer in spirit. It had been rebranded and was now the Maldron.

The road from Oranmore to Claregalway was unusually quiet, but it was Saturday morning. Several roundabouts and a level crossing had to be negotiated, not to mention the new motorway under construction. At the airport, an Aer Arann flight was preparing for take-off and Carnmore Cross had a new set of traffic lights.

The corporate park in Claregalway was mostly unoccupied. Two hares sat by the dried-up fountain. The village primary school was closed that day while the silver spiked sculpture stood sentinel by the church, shimmering in the morning sun. The traffic lights were green, and I had a clear run through the village.

I turned left at Lough George, past the old Connolly Sports building. Now derelict, I remembered a time when it was a hive of activity, turning out sliothars, hurls, helmets, footballs, shinpads, gloves and all kinds of sporting merchandise. A few miles on, the milk-white goalposts of the Annaghdown GAA field came into view.

Round the next corner stood Peggy's Pub. I always wondered what went down in Peggy's but had never been inside. Was there even a Peggy at all? My friend, the Sergeant, was known to frequent it and had given it favourable reviews but had never confirmed or denied the existence of Peggy.

It was around Corndulla that the first sign appeared to announce the upcoming races at Ballinrobe. There was little time to consider the billboards or the racing as I tried to join the line of traffic on the Castlebar road.

I hadn't thought about journeys end. Perhaps I didn't want to think about it. Anything but the thing! I found myself daydreaming of other days when I had driven westwards along that road. Memories of regular Friday evening journeys were still fresh. It was over five years ago now that it had all ended, so abruptly and with such finality.

I had seldom been this way since, and indeed, until yesterday, I had had little reason to think about Mary Rose in the intervening period. Why should I? She had moved on, and I had moved on, gone our separate ways. It had been good while it lasted, but when it ended, it was like a door had slammed shut.

As always, the Trading Post at Cloghanover advertised its cheap fuel and was a hive of activity. Headford by the lake was its usual nondescript self. A poster announced the opening of the new GAA Clubhouse while the plain grey hotel at the crossroads still looked as if not much, bar a few stray foreign fishermen, had come or gone in a long time.

I had memories of the Armagh people who lived further up the main street. I didn't know them, nor had I ever set eyes on them, but a few years ago, when the Orchard footballers were in their pomp, around Easter time, they would hang a large orange flag from the upstairs window where it would remain for the whole summer. There was neither pennant nor person to be seen there today.

A friend of Mary Rose used to own a pub down by the lake. He was a very proper, genteel, impeccably turned out little man. He had a story too. He was living with a Cork woman when last heard of. He had encountered his partner online, and soon afterwards, she had moved in with him accompanied by her two young daughters. He had gone down to Cork with a trailer and brought his new family back. The Cork woman smoked roll-ups often laced with weed. Mary Rose had reservations about this lady and was greatly concerned for her friend. She feared he would be cleaned out. I hadn't had an update on this situation since Mary Rose and myself went our separate ways, but now I wondered what had happened in the meantime between those two strange bedfellows.

Just outside Headford, Galway ends, and Mayo begins. It is a painless, if not seamless, transition. The most noticeable change is that the roads improve almost immediately. Glencorrib is the first village in Mayo, but it has a bare, featureless, almost always deserted, one-horse town kind of look about it. Then comes Cross with its little bubbling river and its air of tidiness and quaintness. The neat little national school is on the left as you come into the village. Its playing pitch is always in pristine condition, well marked out with white painted posts and its green handmade wooden dugouts.

Cross neighbours the Neale, another interesting little village. Typical of Mayo, it has a sizeable stone grotto beside the church and there's a large pyramid on the far side of the village. Yes, a pyramid! It must have been built as a folly, probably at the time of the famine. And, of course, the village also boasts the Pyramid Restaurant. Just outside the village, a bunch of brightly coloured balloons floats in the breeze, above a placard announcing to the world the impending marriage of Mark and Mary.

As Mary and Mark faded from memory, I approached Ballinrobe. Its main claim to fame being that it has the only racecourse in Mayo. The town also has a sense of height about it. On its approach, you are confronted by two grey concrete water towers, like a pair of giant mushrooms on the skyline. At the other end of town stands a tall communications tower bristling with antennae which wouldn't be out of place at the headquarters of MI5. The town centre is usually busy, but there is a grey dereliction on the outskirts where most of the shops sit empty and boarded up. Essentially, the racecourse is the town's saving grace.

I drove slowly up that narrow street past the church. I could see Petals N' Buds was still in business. I used to stop there to buy flowers for Mary Rose. It was a long, brightly lit shop, and the flowers were arranged along one wall. The cash desk and counter were at the rear, and I recalled walking the length of the shop absorbing the fragrances, aromas and the muted colour on the way. The lady would take great care wrapping up the bouquet and was always available to compose the most appropriate message - if you wanted a message.

Beyond Ballinrobe, past the racecourse, there is a narrow, rickety bridge, and you just have to hope you don't meet a vehicle coming the other way. Lough Mask stretches away to the right. Bill, an architect acquaintance, lived somewhere along the lake in a big house with his wife, three daughters, two Pointer dogs and an army of cats. I wondered if he was prepared for the looming recession and guessed that he was.

The radio had been on all the time, but I only listened intermittently. Barack Obama had apparently made a significant pronouncement on future relations with Cuba. A new singing sensation from Scotland had been making all the news in recent days. Susan Boyle was later to become internationally renowned for her music, but now she had been hospitalised, suffering from what was described as exhaustion. The newsreader then announced that an Irish mercenary had been shot dead in Bolivia. Just another day's news. For a time, my thoughts hovered somewhere between Bolivia and Ballinrobe before a new trigger brought Mary Rose back to mind. Memories of driving up this stretch of road on clear frosty winter nights and that haunting old song from long ago, 'Moonlight in Mayo'. I still could see the moonlight lighting up the landscape with its eerie silvery glow.

The blue Corolla was always parked outside the house. Mary Rose would look out over her glasses as I walked past the window.

She would be sitting in the rotating office chair at the computer. She might be chatting online with her brother, the teacher in Fermoy, or her uncle, the priest in Australia. There would be a big fire blazing in the grate. She usually had dinner ready for me. Sometimes if she was in great humour. she would have a bath poured. There would be a few scented candles and maybe a glass of wine sitting on the end of the bath.

In Partry, I turned off the main road and took a left. I recalled the evening Mary Rose and myself had taken a jaunt out this way to a place called the 'Goats Hotel.' There was a story about the place which I had long forgotten. I did remember that there was no hotel there and little sign of goats either. We had just driven out from the Port that time, turned around and headed back.

This was a great road to travel with lots of the typical Mayo landscape, which she used to refer to as beautiful, brown, barren, boggy and lots of other words beginning with 'b'. Next up was a sign for Tourmakeady. I had gone there once with a group of friends and remembered a long walk up to a waterfall.

As I neared my destination, the children of Mary Rose came to mind. Thoughts of them ended my idle reverie and brought me to earth with a bump. The kids were distant, to say the least. There were four of them. The red-haired daughter, Aine, was still in national school at that time. She was forever watching me when she thought I wasn't looking. It was usual for her to go to her room when I was around. Mostly she was off to her father's house at weekends, and I was spared her long silences. The older daughter was in England at college and seldom seen.

The younger son, who was in his last year at school, was a strange complex character and made it very obvious that he didn't like me. He was a smoker, and I suspected a smoker of more than tobacco. Mary Rose refused to believe it even though it was blindingly obvious. The older fellow, a rookie teacher, was quieter and easy to get along with. He didn't smoke. Both spent most of their spare time out of the house.

I was expected to drive the sons here and there as required, mostly to the home of relatives who lived out in the country. I didn't relish these particular errands, but with Mary Rose, it was her way or no way. They also visited their father in Ballyhaunis from time to time, but Mary Rose didn't expect me to do that run.

My eyes were usually drawn to the triangulated mountain, Croagh Patrick, but it was covered in cloud today. A mist had descended as I approached the Port, and visibility was down to about a few hundred metres. The Loftuses were all crisscrossing my mind now, sometimes singularly and at other times in bulk.

I could never understand what her uncle, the priest, was doing in Australia. All the Irish priests I had known on the foreign missions were usually sent to the Philippines, Nigeria and such places. Yet there he was in Ullimaroa, where he had a parish and enjoyed a comfortable lifestyle with a lot of golf included. I wondered if he wore pink jumpers, ran bingo sessions, kept greyhounds or had started a branch of the pioneers over there. He hardly ran pilgrimages to Knock, Lourdes, Fatima or Medjugorje from that remove. I casually wondered if they had equivalent pilgrimages in the Antipodes and whether The Virgin had ever appeared under the Southern Cross.

The Loftus family was a typically big Irish family with lots of roots, branches and tentacles. Her brother, Peter, was a bachelor and often visited Mary Rose. I always associated Peter with dandruff. He was a sour little man and seldom spoke. Peter had the aura of a lost soul and was a big fan of the Glasgow Celtic soccer team. I teased him sometimes about his Scottish heroes and their Irish supporters, known derogatively as 'the weekend Fenians'. He said little, but I knew the evidence was noted to be used against me at a future date. Peter was involved in some sort of clandestine relationship with an in-law from County Carlow. This was a cause of some scandal, but generally it was an off-limits topic within the family.

The other brothers didn't appear as often. There were James the draughtsman, Matt the thatcher, and the good-looking blonde-haired Shane who was a teacher in Fermoy. Shane was great fun and I enjoyed his company very much. Mary Rose was usually at loggerheads with him, so we only saw him occasionally. There was also Mikey the dentist, who had worked in Germany but was now back in Ireland living in Athlone with his Westmeath wife. Mary Rose didn't like the wife and said she was a controller, which was a wonderful irony.

The father and mother lived further down the same road. Every day, Mary Rose would call on her way to work. Mark, the father, was a man of many parts. He had retired several years before, but he still did some voluntary work for the church. In his day, he had worked as an accountant and was a renowned athlete and footballer.

The mother, Elizabeth, was more austere, kept a tight rein on the father and was the boss in that house. When I had visited, I was always offered a seat by the fire, tea would be made and there was a warm welcome. Elizabeth was, in some ways, a role model for Mary Rose.

I passed by a nightclub in the middle of the countryside with its huge, empty car park. We had come this way the evening Mary Rose had brought me to Knock Shrine. We had done the full tour of the shrine on that occasion. She used to go on about the miracle of Knock and the power of prayer. I never dared to disagree. During our tour, we went into several different churches, shrines and basilicas, managing to get in some amount of prayer in each. In all of these places, the sick, the wounded and the bewildered congregated. Nuns and priests wandered around, relaxed and comfortable on home ground. Mary Rose filled a few bottles of holy water from the taps outside before we left. To round that expedition off in an appropriate manner, we called to Ballintubber Abbey on the way back. There were some relatives buried there.

Mary Rose had often hinted that she wanted to marry me. This was her biggest and most persistent dream. I didn't share this aspiration but dared not disagree. I valued my freedom and thought the one marriage I had had was quite enough. But her dream was set in stone. There was no room for negotiation. I had once been taken to see the local parish priest to seek advice on remarrying, but luckily for me, that was as far as it went.

It was drizzling now. I still couldn't see the Reek nor any other mountains. I recalled the day she took me up to that country in the shadow of Nephin. She had shown me where the family home was and took me to a graveyard where most of the Loftuses were buried. We spent some time in that peaceful and scenic place and she got very emotional when she talked about the deaths of her grandparents, recalling these episodes in the greatest detail with a full account of wakes, funerals and burial arrangements down to who dug the graves. She took things like this very much to heart.

I passed under the railway bridge on the edge of town and along past Toby's pub, which now looked empty and uninviting. Two sad-looking Eastern Europeans were carrying sheets of plasterboard from a lorry into a shop which was in the throes of renovation. I wasn't sure whether it was rain or sweat dripping from their Yankees baseball caps.

As I approached the town centre, there were vivid recollections of romantic nights in Westport. We often frequented the Greek restaurant which did the best moussaka in the west, according to herself. Her niece Tracy was a chef there. Afterwards, there would be a visit to Matt Molloys or Morans. In Matt's, there would be big seisuns of music, a packed house and plenty of craic. A lot of

Northern Ireland people seemed to find their way there at weekends. Morans had no music but had a great atmosphere with the patrons packed like sardines into this uniquely Irish setup of a pub with a shop at the front. It was the place to meet a rare character and one often did.

I parked around the back of the house, got out of the car, yawned, scratched myself, stretched myself, fixed my tie and looked at my watch. The town was starting to get busy, and a few tourists wandered in and out of the gift shops. I stood there for a minute in the weak mid-morning sun.

I buttoned my coat and entered by the back door. Inside I could see the family were all there, standing around among clusters of friends, neighbours and colleagues. They regarded me through glazed, unseeing eyes as I shook hands with each of them in turn. In the sitting room lay Mary Rose, looking immaculate as ever but as white as a ghost and as dead as a stone.

Her Irish eyes like beacons shine all in the darkest night
I know their sweet love beams will always fill the world with light
The roses on her cheeks will lend enchantment to the scene
And when shamrocks wear the dew I'll wed my sweet colleen.

The End

Printed in Great Britain
by Amazon

74518637R00068